Charles Maurice Davies

'Verts- Or the Three Creeds

Vol. III

Charles Maurice Davies

'Verts- Or the Three Creeds
Vol. III

ISBN/EAN: 9783337249953

Printed in Europe, USA, Canada, Australia, Japan

Cover: Foto ©Andreas Hilbeck / pixelio.de

More available books at **www.hansebooks.com**

'VERTS;

OR,

THE THREE CREEDS.

THE THREE CREEDS.

've RTS;

OR,

THE THREE CREEDS.

A Novel.

BY

Dr. MAURICE DAVIES,

AUTHOR OF "UNORTHODOX LONDON," "BROAD CHURCH," ETC.

"The Bee and Spider, by a diverse power,
Suck honey and poison from the selfsame flower."

IN THREE VOLUMES.

VOL. III.

LONDON:

TINSLEY BROTHERS, 8, CATHERINE STREET, STRAND.
1876.

LONDON:
SAVILL, EDWARDS AND CO., PRINTERS, CHANDOS STREET,
COVENT GARDEN.

CONTENTS

OF

THE THIRD VOLUME.

’VERTS.

BOOK III.—IN THE VOLUME OF THE BOOK.

CHAPTER I.

THE RELIGION FOR A GENTLEMAN.

THE duties of life have so thickened, upon Mr. and Mrs. Alec Lund that they find no time for letter-writing or diary-keeping; and their story has to be rounded out by an abstract narrator in the ordinary third person.

Alec—for we must assume the liberty thus to abridge his cognomen—has sunk down into the journalist pure and simple; and no avocation is more exacting. His only wish is that there were thirty-six hours instead of twenty-four in each working day; and he adopts the expedient so much in favour among members of the Fourth Estate, of lengthening those days by stealing a few hours from the night, my boys.

Elsie laughs, very significantly indeed, at the tactics he adopts in reference to theological matters. He generally preserves the most rigid and mysterious silence. He seems to have pleased nobody by the change he has made; but he makes believe violently to have pleased himself. Mrs. Fane is disappointed that he has not become a devotee like herself. It is a terrible fact to narrate, but he seldom goes to church. He makes the newspaper his excuse; and no doubt a daily paper does stand in the way of High Mass, which Mrs. Fane, like every 'vert, principally affects; but he could go to early mass if he would only turn out betimes; and of course there is no late work on Saturday night.

"Alec dear, you don't seem to have found that resting-place for the sole of your foot which you expected to realize in the Catholic Church," said Elsie; she not having made the plunge herself, but waiting calmly on the bank to see what is going to happen.

"I don't in the least know why you should say so. I am perfectly serene."

"Very serene."

"What do you mean by saying very serene? Is it not so?"

"Oh, I daresay; but——"

"But what?"

"It's rather serene than exciting."

"Religion is not excitement."

"So the goody tract says, I know—one of those I used to read while T. and P. were going on, I think."

"Hold your tongue, and go to the baby."

For there is a baby; and whenever Alec wants to cut short an argument, theological or otherwise, he vows his son and heir is crying. He says Elsie does not seem at home with the infant; accuses her of mislaying it sometimes, and tells people her legs are so bony that she gives the poor child incipient bed-sores when she dandles it on her maternal lap.

Mr. William Llewellyn went in bodily fear of Mr. Moddle, until he heard of that gentleman's secession and subsequent rejection by Mrs. Fane. Then he triumphed meanly over him at first, but soon after the two were fast friends again; and now it is a mystery what mischief the pair are brewing. They are always together; and lookers-on, who proverbially see most of the game, aver that they are not much more devoted sons of the Church than Mr. Lund himself. When they are taxed with disloyalty, they are much too pronounced in their assurances of undying attachment. These very ardent disciples always make one suspicious. No doubt Judas Iscariot was the most forward of the twelve.

In the meantime the Roman propagandism continues. Father Blank has his hands full; Father Pugin finds his brethren every now and then flitting, and bears it philosophically enough; while, haunting the debateable land between the English and Roman Communions, hovers the impalpable presence of Presbyter Anglicanus. The Ritualists have raised a spirit which they cannot lay; and in vain the so-called "moderate" men among the party become Protestants in turn, and disavow all connexion with the obnoxious Presbyter. Advanced men cannot assume the virtues of the via media. Their very essence is to be in extremes.

"What is going to become of your unfortunate Establishment, Elsie?" said Alec, one Saturday night; which was about the only occasion when he and his wife could have anything like a confab. When he was not roasting her about the baby, he generally took it out on the subject of "her" Establishment, as he termed it.

"Nay, I am innocent of establishments, as you know. Since I gave up my scheme of seceding to the Particular Baptists, I have forsworn all organizations. My mother is my model churchwoman now."

"Because of no church. Lucus à non lucendo."

"Very much so."

"But, Elsie," said Alec, very seriously, "can you bear to feel and live alone in these matters?"

"Do you remember Keble's beautiful words?—I quote them from memory:—

> "'Why should we faint, and fear to live alone,
>   Since all alone, so Heaven has willed, we die?
> Not even the nearest heart, most like our own,
>   Knows half the reasons why we smile or sigh.'"

"I have, as you know, out-grown Keble."

"Nominally, yes; but I don't think you have, really. Alec dear, you are breaking through that hitherto impenetrable veil of mystery with which you have so far surrounded yourself. Tell me—I think you ought to—are you happy in your new faith?"

"Why ought I to?"

"That very question is also ungenerous—almost unkind. Ought not a husband to tell a wife all about these subjects, unless he finds she has done anything to make her unworthy of confidence—and I have not done that, have I, Alec?"

"Elsie, how can you ask? Certainly not."

"Then do speak openly to me. Speak as you used to do in old, unbelieving days, when you very nearly converted me to your creed of negation. You have surely as much at least to say on behalf of your now more positive form of belief?"

"To tell a person to talk is, as you well know, generally the most effectual way of shutting that person up. But I will be communicative, Elsie. You know my reticence does not proceed from the cause you pretended to suppose, don't you?"

"Distrust of me, you mean? Well, yes, I hope I do know that, because I am so thoroughly conscious that I never gave you cause for distrust. Let me help you to break the ice, for I know what great bashful creatures men are in these cases.   You do *not* feel so comfortable in your new faith as you expected?"

"Partly that——"

"Only partly?"

"I am comfortable, and yet not comfortable."

"Explain."

"I feel rather like a man who has taken a pleasant narcotic, but not swallowed quite enough of the drug to make him altogether unconscious.   His remaining vitality puts in a silent protest against his partial lethargy."

"So you are a Protestant after all?"

"In that sense, I am.   The vulgar objections against the Catholic system—I mean Uncle Sam's, and the T. and P. diatribes—are, well—are just what you might suppose them, from their source, to be."

"Fibs?"

"I always use a stronger monosyllable for Patty's unctuous inventions.   But then you were never likely to be led away by the diatribes of Mr. Morphine and his party."

" I always looked upon them as the spiteful inventions of a jealous and hostile sect."

" And there you are right. No, the Catholic system does not violate morality, truckle to worldliness, or sap the authority of conscience. It is, in fact, the embodied conscience, as I hoped it would be."

" And in this respect you are comfortable under its régime ?"

" Could I be otherwise ?"

" Can I guess what it is that qualifies your comfort, and prevents you from feeling the full satisfaction you had expected ?"

" I think it very probable that you can."

" Shall I try ?"

" Do."

" You do not find that this embodied conscience is checked by what Tyndall calls co-operant reason."

" I do not. That is just the important

factor that I find omitted from the process."

" I thought so."

" I remember the passage you so aptly cite. It occurs in Tyndall's 'Address on the Scientific Use of the Imagination.' Now I pushed the Professor's argument one step farther than he himself carried it. If we were to call in the faculty of Imagination to aid our scientific investigations into the infinitely distant nebula or the infinitely minute molecule; so, surely, we might invoke a corresponding faculty, now called Faith rather than Imagination—but each covered by the significant word *Vorstellung*—to aid us in seeing the invisible; to be literally the substance of things hoped for, the evidence of things not seen."

" And your faith does this?"

" It does; but it demands infallibility for its conclusions, just as the Church which is the embodied Faith—the embodied conscience—does."

" And you would term those conclusions

no more than reverent hypotheses until confirmed by an appeal to reason ?"

" Yes."

" Then I can quite understand that, so
far, you are no true son of the Church ; but,
Alec——"

" Yes."

" You must have known all that before
you joined the Church."

" I did ; but for the moment my
emotional nature was uppermost, and
directly you allow that to be the case, Rome
is your only logical resource."   .

" Not Ritualism ?"

" No. If I elect to throne conscience,
whether individual or collective, supreme
above all else, I must accept its dicta in
every particular, whether of Church government, or in cases of conscience specifically
so termed."

" You allude to the supremacy of the
Pope ?"

" I do. If it were possible that the
Church could tell me to accept the supre-

macy of the Grand Llama of Thibet, or Mrs. Girling the Shaker Mother, I must obey."

"And there you perceive a sphere for the exercise of co-operant reason."

"I do."

"Then why not seek it among the sects?"

"Because no sect enables me to exercise it ad libitum. Every one says 'Thus far and no further.' If I am to stop inquiry anywhere, I will stop it at the first step. It is idle, illogical to arrest it afterwards."

"Then you do *not* find, Alec, that the Catholic Religion is the religion for gentlemen—only for poor and ignorant people?"

"Yes I do. It is emphatically the religion for a gentleman or a gentlewoman.'"

"Mrs. Fane to wit."

"Exactly. For one who requires the culture of external life to be carried up into the higher domain of spiritual matters, and who—well, who does not want to think out things too much—it is the very system of systems."

"And is not this the creed of the majority?"

"Why, Elsie," replied Alec, with a merry laugh, "we seem to be turning the tables, and you seeking to convert me. Yes," he continued, "I think it very likely the majority of people are in that condition of mental feebleness; but, I ask myself, ought they to be so—nay, *can* they honestly remain so in days when the schoolmaster is abroad?"

"A grave question, truly."

"And if they cannot honestly shut their eyes to intellectual facts, may not such dishonesty extend beyond the sphere of intellect and vitiate morality?"

"Do you find it does? You are behind the scenes."

"I do *not* find it. The T. and P. libels are vulgar lies, but then——"

"What then?"

"The system is not triumphant now. I

distrust the tendency should it emerge again from its present position as a persecuted faith."

" Very mildly persecuted."

" Yes, very mildly persecuted, but still not supreme. Your only test of Catholicism is to view it where it has been the dominant system."

" And then ?"

" Then you have to trust the testimony of history which may misrepresent facts."

" Ah! then I can understand the state of chaos you are in ; but what I cannot under-stand still is why you have not said this all to me ages ago."

" Ages ago! Why, I am not a three months' old infant in the Church yet."

" But æons are not made up of days and years in these matters. Eternity may be crowded into a moment."

" That is another idea that often crosses my consciousness too, Elsie. Come close to me, wife, for it is a notion one can only speak of with bated breath. Eternity may supervene on time at any moment, and then it would be so supremely important to feel rightly on these matters. I often ask myself, Is not conscience, as Bishop Butler teaches us, by right despotic? Are not all these suggestions of the lower faculties—this protest of the intellect, this murmur of private judgment—only anarchical rebellion of the lower against the higher constituents in our nature?"

"And yet, Alec," said the wife, harping, womanlike, upon the one string, "you could allow me to run that fearful risk of finding time merge in eternity without my feeling right upon these supreme subjects."

"Do not be cruel. It is not with a woman as with a man on such subjects. You do not find these protests so strong, I fancy. You have more of your mother's nature. She can sit down and accept all in pure faith without the intrusion of logic. I so often ask myself, 'Is it *not* an intrusion, is it not a case of men rushing in where angels fear to tread when questionings thus desecrate the sanctuary of faith ?' "

"Can you not rest and be thankful, then, Alec? Can you not put the questions from you by main force, and develop pure faith only?"

"Could you, Elsie?"

"I have never tried, never been in the position where it became my duty to try."

"Will you cross the Rubicon—come over to where I am stretching out my hands from the opposite side, and then see whether you can do it? If you can, I should feel confidence that I could."

"And if not?"

"Then, to be consistent, I must re-turn——"

"To what? Anglicanism?"

"No; to a position beyond the creeds and Churches altogether."

"And leave me folded in the Church, perhaps. That would be a strange reversal of our present position, and one less natural than this."

He remained silent, seeming to be working out the problem in his own consciousness. Elsie continued—

"I really think it is better that, for a time at least, we should each remain as we are. We may serve as a check on one another. Folded together in Rome we may turn into a mere pair of devotees, as once, recollect, we were a pair of sceptics."

"And now are sundered widely as the poles by the fatal 'religious difficulty.' Is it not so?"

"Scarcely. There is this very remarkable feature in our case—but then, of course, we have been remarkable people all along, have we not?—that differences, which would be fatal to others, are trifles light as air to us. Why should it not be so? Why cannot people agree to differ? Why lose our tempers about matters of faith?"

"Philosophers do not."

"Then the majority of human nature must be fools, Alec."

"It is a terrible conclusion to arrive at;

but, I fear, a very logical one. On these matters of religious and political belief the very large majority of us *are* fools."

"The more glorious our state of exception. I well recollect that, when my father's difficulties first threatened him, or, at least, when I was first permitted to know of their existence, I used to fall into deep fits of dejection at the bare idea of having to face difficulties. Then occasionally came a lucid interval. I would reduce life, so to say, to its actual requirements. What did we absolutely need in order to live, and even enjoy life? How much that we now looked upon in the light of necessity was really the merest superfluity. Abstract that, and how easy the conditions of philosophic existence were. Happiness, I used to think, might be considered to lie, not so much in the golden mean, certainly not in the stratum above it, but in a voluntary de-gradation—so to say —I mean, of course, in the strict etymological sense of the term, not in the conventional usage of it."

"I understand."

"May we not apply something of the same analogy to these questions that now agitate us, or agitate those around us, and sometimes send a faint ripple over the serenity of our lives? Given the grand fundamental of all religion, it is extraordinary on what a slender addition of externals the spirit can live and energize."

"Like the hind on his oatmeal porridge, in contrast with our delicate dinners à la Russe."

"Precisely."

So it was arranged, as the practical result of this and similar colloquies, that each should retain his or her position; Alec Lund enjoying his "religion for a gentleman," and his wife remaining true to the traditions of philosophic Anglicanism. The same position was also exactly repeated in Mr. William Llewellyn and his wife. Mr. Llewellyn was soon advanced to the post of sacristan at the suburban church near which he dwelt; and there was enough in

the petits soins demanded by his office to fill
up his time and prevent him from wasting
his superabundant leisure any longer upon
his son-in-law. His wife worshipped in-
discriminately before his gaily-bedizened
altar, or in the whitewashed sanctuary of
the next Dissenting Chapel. It was all one
to her. The result was that the idea of an
ecclesiastical Happy Family was perhaps as
nearly realized as possible in this essentially
Church Militant condition of things.

Few outsiders were aware of the change
in Alec Lund’s creed. He never, even in
his most unbelieving days, descended to
vituperation of creed or system, or coldly
criticised a practice that differed from his
own. He really was what he professed to
be, a religious man without religion—that
is without any formulated religion. There
are more such men extant than we imagine.
When any one twitted him with his
scepticism in those bygone days he was
generally content to smile on them and
quote, whether in his nest on Dovecot Hill

or his smoking-chair in the Vicar's Close
at Zoar, Tennyson's words from *In
Memoriam :*—

> " There lives more faith in honest doubt,
>   Believe me, than in half the creeds."

If ever he drifted into orders, he said,
which was not likely, he would elevate Saint
Thomas to be head of his hagiology. He
could discern no rebuke in the remark made
to that outspoken doubter on the superior
blessedness of those who believed without
having seen.

"Not only," he would remark, " is it a
condition of mental emasculation which I
do not ambition, but it is one which I simply
cannot accept or comprehend. To ask me
to believe a thing of which I have no proof,
is to ask me to hear with my eyes or see
with my ears. I have no faculty for it.
Faith is one thing ; credulity another."

Surely a curious psychological problem it
was, then, to see this man forcibly put from
him private judgment and elect to guide his
steps by pure faith. The process was

simple enough. It was the double one that sent the two Newmans flying off divergently into the uttermost realms of theological space. He felt that his conclusions, pushed to their legitimate lengths, must land him in blank Atheism; and he could not face that possibility. Frederick William Newman's "Phases of Faith," he said, was the most logical book ever written; and its only antidote was John Henry Newman's "Apologia."

Whether informed of Lund's changed creed or not, one of his newspaper confrères said to him in the course of conversation, while the leader-writers were awaiting the arrival of their chief—

" I say, old fellow, what change has come over the spirit of your dream? Ignoring all ideas of Catholic Aggression, you call the Cardinal 'his Eminence,' and it seems to me, when I read your proofs, as though you could cut off your right hand rather than suffer yourself to omit the ' Right Reverend' from Monsignor's appellation."

"I simply call things by their right names. To me it seems the height of bad taste to do otherwise. I would dub Dr. Cumming the 'Right Worshipful,' if any respectable authority invested him with the title."

"Is that all?"

"Is not that enough?"

"Perhaps so; only I don't think you always did it. Indeed, I am sure a reference to the filed copy would show you did not."

"Don't trouble to refer. Simply accept my explanation that I have grown older and wiser."

"Older and wiser, eh?" and his interlocutor looked askance at Alec in a very knowing way indeed; but Alec could be inscrutable as the Sphinx when it suited his purpose.

Had he grown older and wiser simultaneously? The question would recur. Had he not rather administered a very powerful narcotic to one portion of his curiously compounded nature, from the effects of which bland sedative his judgment was ever and anon fitfully awakening, until drugged to sleep again by the sensuous adjuncts of his new creed? It was very beautiful; and when the influence was full upon him, as on the occasion of his rare presence at High Mass, or when Elsie would kneel with him amid the deepening evening shadows at the sweet Benediction Service, he felt that the spell was indeed a potent one, and he would not if he could emancipate himself from the happy thraldom. If only his wife were at one with him on this as on all other topics, he would, he thought, be perfectly happy.

If! And yet he took no steps to "convert" her—that was how he phrased it. It was precisely as a man might act who had swallowed the pleasant opiate, yet would not administer the same to one in whom he felt interest. He did not repel her advance to him, but he did not encourage it, for he knew that a word from him would have been all-sufficient, and she would have

made the step on the strength of his
assurance that the step ought to be made.
He dared not suggest it. Mrs. Fane took
him continually to task on the subject.

"Alec," she said, "I am disappointed in
you. I hoped much from you in the way
of proselytizing, and you suffer even your
own wife to remain a heretic."

He remained silent, answering only with
a significant smile.

"You mean Elsie is not an easy one to
convert. But you should try on easier
subjects first. I have converted everybody
about me, from the maid who washes the
dishes up to the young lady-help who
arranges my hair. I have invested a small
fortune in Milner's 'End of Religious Controversy,' and give it to everybody who can
read."

"Elsie is very far beyond that."

"I believe if you would only make one
more journey to your bijou cathedral city,
or your mythical Welsh estates, I could
convert her myself. You positively seem

to me to keep her back from joining the Church."

" I do nothing at all."

" The most effectual method of putting a stumbling-block in her way. I shall really have a word with the Cardinal."

" I wouldn't trouble; because the whole college and the Pope to boot couldn't make me a propagandist unless I liked."

" You are but a poor Catholic after all, I fear, Alec."

" I am, at all events, what you made me, my very dear mother in the faith."

"Don't call me mother, you prodigal. I won't own you. No, but, Alec, seriously I do feel the awkwardness of Elsie's being the only Protestant amongst us. Amy is quite unhappy at the gulf that exists between Elsie and herself."

" Pay my wife the quarter's wages, or give her the usual notice with promise of a character, and you can exchange her for one of the faithful at your pleasure."

"Don't talk idiotically. We should not

part with Elsie, as you know, of our own free will, though she joined the Shakers. My only objection to that baby is that I know it will one day be the cause of separation between governess and pupil."

"But Amy is nearly finished, as they say, is she not?"

"Alas, yes. What shall I do when the actual coup de grâce has been given?"

"Take to nursing my son and heir. You may convert him, perhaps, if you give him some consecrated pap, or drop a soupçon of holy water into his Maw's Feeding Bottle."

"Poor little fellow! He would suffer agonies."

"What, from *eau bénit!* And you call yourself a daughter of the Church. Poor Pius the Ninth! His foes are those of his own household."

It was the little rift within the lute, however, and no one could be more acutely conscious of its existence than Alec Lund himself. In a hundred little unexpected acts and words of daily life the divergence of thought and feeling between husband and wife became constantly more apparent. He felt conscious that she was dragging him back to Anglicanism, since he studiously avoided attracting her towards his own position. What should he do? To abandon that position would be mean and vacillating. To adopt Mrs. Fane's suggestion would be only reasonable, and yet from that course he shrank with an aversion that was perhaps constitutional. What middle course was there?

This. He would wait and work. He would forswear thought on this engrossing topic. Let Elsie see all sides of Catholicism, he remaining neutral; and then let her act on her own judgment, to stay or make the change he had made.

As it was they visited all the quiet retreats, the houses of charity, and numerous works of beneficence in Catholic London. When the baby was arrived at due months —not years—of discretion, they even stole a week from his society, and did the like in Paris. This practical aspect of Popery, told greatly with Elsie. She saw how the system descended into the very minutiæ of daily life, not only in the regimen of the confessional, for which she had no great taste, though she did not share the ordinary Protestant objections, because she thought them insular and often vulgar. Not only so, but in responding to the little needs and necessities of daily spiritual life she saw the Catholic system to be very fertile of re-source. The very ringing of Angelus, or the booming of the big church-bell when the host was elevated, spoke to people outside the church, in the fields and busy streets as to what was going on inside those consecrated walls.

"Your religion seems to follow you out from church into the world, Alec," she said. "Mine waits for me to come into church and seek it."

"Yours and mine, Elsie! Why do these objectionable pronouns exist to mark a difference between you and me in this respect?"

Then Elsie would collapse, and sink into impenetrable silence. She would not let him know what was going on within her heart. As long as the meum and tuum existed, they should be rigidly marked off, and no chance word suffered to betray any possible leaning towards a fusion of the two terms.

Then Catholic hospitality and gaiety were tried. Receptions at the Cardinal's, luncheons with Monsignor, visits to religious houses, and to the salons of the Catholic aristocracy succeeded each other with rapidity. Again was Elsie fain to confess that the Catholic religion was emphatically the religion for a gentleman. There was a culture bound up with the creed which, in other systems, appeared to exist, where it did exist, rather in spite of it. She did not mind conceding so much to Alec, but then she immediately ruined the concession by asking what had this to do with Catholi-

cism quâ Catholicism? "I want something
to guide my conduct and calm my spirit,
not merely to satisfy my intellectual crav-
ings, or respond to my sense of taste."

So it was the fissure widened beneath
their feet, and each of them felt that any
chance event might knock all the philosophy out of them at a moment's notice.

A common ground on which they could
meet without, as it appeared, running the
risk of collision, was their mutual taste for
literary, and especially classical studies.
This circumstance of equality formed a distinguishing mark of this somewhat excep-
tional pair. Generally speaking, religion
forms really the only arena at all partaking
of an intellectual character on which husband and wife meet; and this may account
for the way in which some men dispose of
the matter, as being altogether a woman's
"idle tale." Intellectual and literary pursuits seemed to form a safe sphere enough
for interchange of ideas between Alec Lund
and his wife; but even here, as if to show

how curiously religion does follow us into every detail of life, possible pitfalls would every now and then display themselves. While Elsie translated an Ode of Horace, Alec would English a monastic hymn, and each was disposed to ask the other for an endorsement of excellence on behalf of the secular or sacred poet respectively.

"Your mind, Alec, resembles a palimpsest."

"You have been getting up that word for a Spelling Bee. Would you mind explaining, Madame Interrogatrix?"

"Just as those old hymnodists rubbed down the classical texts to write their quaint old ditties on the same parchment, so, in your brain, the sacred seems to have well nigh displaced the secular, though the old classical vein will crop up occasionally."

"Yes, there are methods, you know, of cleaning these palimpsests, and recovering the classical original, but at the expense— mind that, Elsie—at the expense of the sacred superscription."

"Which things are an allegory, you mean to say."

"And rather a striking one, are they not?"

"Very."

"If you were to scrub my hymns off me, and leave only the classical original of old Zoar times, would you be satisfied?"

"And if you could rub all the Horace off me, and make me only a 'religious' young matron, would *you* be satisfied?"

"I don't know."

"Nor do I."

"I tell you what I have a great mind to do," continued Alec Lund.

"What?"

"Turn money-grubber. Not care about you, or about these bothering questions, but simply enthrone Plutus as my chief deity."

"Call him Mammon, as you represent the theological side of the question, please. I may want Plutus myself by-and-by."

"Well, enthrone Mammon as the chief deity in my Pantheon, and simply try how much money I could make for the sake of Plantagenet, there."

He pointed to the cradle, where his infant son lay. The child's name was not Plantagenet, but Alec liked to confer on him these and sundry other lofty titles. He had already begun to chaff that most immature fragment of humanity. It was his "nature to" he said.

"And do you know what I have considerably more than half a mind to do too ?"

"Tell me."

"Concentrate my energies wholly and solely on Plantagenet."

"Plantagenet seems to be in luck's way ; but how ?"

"Beyond the care and attention which a mother must bestow on her offspring, I will devote myself to the adornment of Plantagenet's person."

"He hasn't got much person to adorn at present."

"I will concentrate my energies on that

minute focus. The more merit in making so much of so little. He shall set the fashion to the infants of the suburb. His perambulator shall be the cynosure of neighbouring nursemaids. His hoods shall be the loudest, his long robes the most emphatic in the neighbourhood. We shall be able to afford it, you know, when you have given up everything for money-grubbing."

"Exactly."

" Then, too, I shall vacate my post with Amy Fane, so as further to fix my whole care and thought on this one sublime pursuit—my infant à-la-mode."

" Don't talk of the child as if he were beef at an eating-house."

" It's beneath my matronly dignity to be acting as daily governess now ; and as you are going to give up all mundane pursuits for money-grubbing, there will be no more need for me to sacrifice my dignity on the altar of Plutus. I told you I should want that heathen deity."

3—2

"What fools we are!"

"Please speak for yourself, and there will be no chance of a dissentient voice. Yes; I think for you to talk of money-grubbing when you neglect as you do a fortune lying at your feet, is rather rich."

"I neglect a fortune?"

"You."

"How?"

"Where is the active lawyer who was to supplant Sheppard and instal us en grand seigneur at Topaz? Where any signs of your striving to regain possession of our lapsed inheritance in the Principality?"

"The Spanish Castles?"

"No; it's vice versâ in all other respects with us now; let us change sides in this matter too. You call those possessions by the airy title of Spanish Castles. I give them the substantial appellation of the Mudwalla Estates."

"If you want a pleasant outing on a wild-goose chase, do as I did, go to Wales and hunt after them."

" No, I wouldn't do that, because we have such a vague clue to go upon. Do you know what my advice is in reference to this quest ?"

" No ; what ?"

" Consult a medium."

" What, are you 'verted to Spiritualism ?"

" Never mind. That is my advice. Let us consult a medium, or rather it would be my advice, only——"

" What ?"

" I'm frightened to go alone."

" I'll come with you."

" No you won't. You dare not ?"

" Why ?"

" The Pope forbids it."

That was an instance of the kind of mine that was constantly being sprung when least expected. On this occasion it was all in fun and was palpably led up to by Elsie herself; but there were occasions when the explosion was not so agreeable.

" I have method in my apparent madness, and Sheppard is not quite such a fool as he

looks you know, Elsie. Shall I tell you
why we are not tackling Edward Llewellyn
in re the Topaz Farm?"

"Yes, of course. Why haven't you told
me already?"

"I reserved it for the occasion when you
should accuse us of lethargy. I knew it
would come. Now why do you think we
wait?"

"'To give him rope enough,' you would
say."

"Yes; but I never contemplated his
taking such a prodigious allowance. He
has pulled down the old Farm and is
building a magnificent mansion there."

"That was always his plan; a sort of royal
road to the deanery and palace."

"But fancy that astute lawyer being so
besotted as to build now, when he ought to
be quite certain his title will be disputed."

"Do you think Uncle Edward *is* so clever
a lawyer as we once fancied?"

"No. He is a very third-rate rascal;
and if he were not backed up by Sixty-per-

cent. Sam, he would come to grief sooner. Sam shows more talent because he hedges with piety; but how it is the two are such fools as to go in for bricks and mortar, when the title-deeds of Topaz are clearly so much waste paper is more than I can understand."

" Perhaps Uncle Edward feels some distraction necessary, just as you do when you take to money-grubbing, or I when I resolve that Plantagenet shall set the infantile modes for the suburb."

" His difficulties are scarcely theological' ones, though."

" Ecclesiastical ones. The Bishop and Dean are to him what the Pope and the Cardinal——"

Another pitfall. Elsie was plump into it on this occasion. There was nothing for it but to flounder out as best she might; so she resumed——

" I am half disposed to pity that man, ruthless as his conduct has been to me and mine. Knowing, as he must do, that the hue-and-cry is after Percy, and that any moment he may be caught and——"

"Say it; don't hesitate. I rather enjoy mentioning it, since I had such a narrow shave. Caught and hanged, you mean?"

"Yes; considering the agony he must suffer night and day with that thought weighing upon him, one can scarcely wonder that he expends his energies on bricks and mortar, or anything that will distract him from the one corroding anxiety."

"Do you think that, in his lawyer-like mind some vague sense of justice makes him determine to spend on the estate some few thousands of the accumulations he has made from it? That is really the only explanation I can give."

"Perhaps."

"Directly we do move, we shall drop down on him relentlessly for all the back rents."

"You will?"

"Of course."

"Then I see it all."

"See what?"

"Uncle Sam. He is advising Uncle Edward to adopt the method you call hedging with piety. When it does come into court, he will say, not in so many legal words, perhaps, but in a suggested moral, 'See, I have spent all this money on the place. I yield it up to these young people as soon as ever their title is proved. Can I do more? Will the court be hard upon me under the circumstances?' Do you not think that is the kind of game he is playing?"

"Very likely."

"Then if Percy is taken that will be another bitter ingredient in his cup. People will exclaim, 'Poor, good, troubled man!' Really, Alec, I begin to read my relatives more plainly than ever. I think among the numerous avocations opened up to women in these times, there is one that we most injudiciously omit."

"What is that?"

"The police."

"And why so?"

"This *reading*, as I term it, would be useful. I feel sure I could have found Percy before this."

"I think we shall manage it without your assistance."

"I don't know what you have been doing, Alec," said Mr. William Llewellyn, appearing at the door, "but you are—to use the language of the light-fingered gentry—'wanted' by a policeman."

"Where?"

"He's waiting outside. Shall I show him in?"

"Please."

It was Alec's old friend the sergeant, and he told him he had just stepped in, quite in an unbusinesslike way, to say they were going to arrest Percy that night. Would he like to go?"

"Where?"

"I may mention it before the lady, I suppose, sir? It's out of order, but we've worked together before. He's not in London, but lying hid, where of all places do you suppose?"

" Where?"

He answered in a sort of stage-whisper— " Zoar."

CHAPTER II.

RUN TO EARTH.

THE summons which Alec Lund received from the police to make a night-journey with them, and be present at the scene of a murder and prospective arrest, was a far from unusual one for him. In his capacity of descriptive writer on the daily paper to the staff of which he now belonged, he continually had to make these mysterious peregrinations; so much so that the police got to look upon him almost as one of themselves, and would have felt almost lonely without him. They expected some reference in his articles to the active and intelligent officers who had the case in charge; and there had been so much said on the opposite side in reference to their dilatoriness in catching the Zoar murderer that they were doubly anxious to have him on this account, as well as for his intimate acquaintance with the locality and the person who was wanted. Alec too felt a strange fascination luring him on to hound down the man who had so nearly brought him to the gallows.

There is something wildly adventurous in thus dashing through the country in the quiet night; and Alec Lund, whose dignity required that he should ensconce himself in a first-class carriage at Paddington, used that dignified retirement as a sort of salon and sleeping-room, adjourning every now and then for a station or two to the second-class compartment where the executive kept vigil, and smoked like veritable locomotives themselves.

"That was a plant, then, sergeant, I suppose—the riverside address Moddle gave Mrs. Fane for Percy's whereabouts?"

"No; that was true enough. He did live for some time at the Crab Tree Inn, Fulham; and a beautiful place it was for throwing us off the scent. He went there as a boating man bent on watching the tides and currents of the river; so his loafing about excited no suspicion at the place. It's no unusual spot for such loungers, I fancy."

"Then Moddle gave him warning when Mrs. Fane refused him, I suppose."

"Yes; women always spoil these things. There was valuable time lost then. If she had come off to Scotland Yard directly she got that Crab Tree address instead of lolloping about to dress herself, we should have got there before Moddle. As it was the bird was flown."

"And Moddle?"

"We've got our eye upon him."

"Of course. That's what you all say. Make a clean breast of it, sergeant, and confess he caught you napping, and has got clear away."

"Well, that's something like it too; but still we've got a clue to him."

"Yes, that's about the change you ring.

You've always either got your eye on a fellow or got a clue to his whereabouts; but nothing ever comes of it, my dear old boy, nothing comes of it."

"Not much sometimes, I must confess. Still we must keep up appearances."

"Confess you're duffers. Own that the French police beat you all to pieces."

"We may be duffers, or may not," replied the sergeant, waxing a little irate; "but as for them French fellows, I've worked a job or two with them, and they're all palaver and politeness. No, give me English officers—constables, I mean—with (don't let this go further) French superiors. That's where the shoe pinches. Our superiors, and especially our detectives *are* duffers, if you like. The men will go any where, and do anything, if properly led."

"Englishmen always will."

"Right you are again, sir," said the sergeant, who was before all things patriotic, and suffered from perfectly painful attacks of esprit de corps. " Right you are; and if we had only had a little brains at work in town and country, and a little facility of communication between the two, the right man would have been lagged at first, and you spared that terrible trial."

" By the right man, meaning this man."

" The man we're after, of course. It don't want no judge or jury to tell us he *is* the right man."

" No," replied Lund; " and yet I am glad the process of judge and jury will have to be gone through in his case as in mine, instead of the jurisdiction of Judge Lynch being recognised. Speaking from my own experience, I would rather have been lynched on the spot by the mob who believed I had killed the poor girl, than suffer the daily, hourly agony of waiting for the trial, and the trial itself."

" Ha !" said the sergeant, meditatively, between two long whiffs at his pipe, " I don't quite feel that. You never tried Judge Lynch, sir."

"And you never tried the other sort of judge. It's all very well for you to stand in the Court with your hat on, a privilege nobody else is allowed, and your white cotton gloves, which always wash too long in the fingers, and to shout 'silence' when nobody is making any noise, and call witnesses by every name but their own——"

"Thank *you*, sir."

"But it's another thing to see judge and jury sitting there in the most cold-blooded way with your life in their hands; to listen to the opposing counsel and his witness distorting every circumstance so as to make it tell against you, and not to be able to open your mouth in self-defence; to see your own advocate even looking askance as the damning evidence crops up bit by bit—to feel a sort of fear that he will throw up your case and leave you to be hung like a dog—that's pleasant, isn't it?"

"Very. But you didn't happen to be in the Park that particular day in 1866, when the mob pulled down the railings, did you?"

"No, I did not. Why?"

"Because you would have seen how much of Judge Lynch's delicate attention our D division underwent, before they drew their truncheons. If you had happened to be there, I don't think you would have envied their position."

"I don't for a moment suppose so either. I only compared its merits with those of a slow trial before the other judge."

"I should prefer the slow process myself, sir," remarked the sergeant, who was a great man for terse remarks. Soon afterwards the train stopped at Bristol, where they had an early breakfast, and Lund retired, when they started again, to collect his thoughts, and possibly freshen himself with a final sleep before the train deposited them at Zoar.

Nobody was up except one particularly sleepy porter at the station and one equally somnolent policeman in the High Street, as this unusually large party emerged from the railway and made the echoes ring through the empty streets with the tramp of their heavy boots. Policemen's boots must differ essentially from those of ordinary mortals, if one may judge by the sonorous clank they make upon the pavement even in the daytime. The drowsy policeman recognised their reverberations at once, and was wide awake to receive the "Lunnon" police, whose advent no doubt had been announced by telegraph. His eyes appeared staring out of his head when the sergeant told him—what had not been entrusted to the wire—that the reputed murderer was most certainly in their midst. Now was a chance for the Zoar police distinguishing themselves and rubbing off at once the stigma that dreadful metropolitan press had cast upon them for letting Percy Llewellyn escape so easily. The country papers were not so severe. There are always wheels within wheels working to tone down the asperities of local prints in reference to constituted authorities; but the country police are fair game for London journalists, who seldom spare them.

"A quiet sort of place, at the best of times, sir," said the reflective sergeant to Alec Lund, as they passed the old house in the High Street.

"Yes; there is a good deal of still life in Zoar. It is a place that requires you to understand it in order to enjoy yourself."

"That I can quite believe, sir."

"See, sergeant, that is the house where the poor girl lived for whose murderer we are searching. Her mother, I believe, lives there still."

"*In*-deed, sir!" replied the sergeant, directing the attention of his two silent coadjutors to the place, and emphasizing the first syllable of his interjection, as if he thought the information very important.

"And the large red-brick house three doors off is where Mr. William Llewellyn, my father-in-law, lived, and where my wife was born."

" *In*-deed, sir !" and he booked the facts this time, utterly irrelevant as they were.

When they got to the middle of the market-place, and Alec Lund once more stopped to point out with pride the old cathedral looking more venerable than ever among the morning mists, and the crumbling arches leading up to the churchyard green and the Bishop's palace respectively, he found the sergeant no longer sympathetic, but quite inaccessible to all ideas of romance.

" There, sergeant—a grand old pile, is it not ?"

" Commodious, sir, no doubt; in fact, I should think, if there was any Dissent at all here, it must be out of proportion to the requirements of the congregation. And— you'll excuse me mentioning it, sir, as I see you feel an interest in this spot—the place strikes me generally as being out of repair —dilapidated like."

That commonplace observation appeared to Alec Lund to involve such an abyss of

bathos that he could not bear to pursue the
subject farther.   He therefore suggested
that valuable time was being lost, and proposed that they should adjourn at once to
the town-hall on the other side of the
market-place—a low, evil-looking building
which had infinitely greater attractions for
the sergeant because it was flanked by one
more dissipated-looking still, from which
hung a red lamp labelled " Police Station,"
and whereinto the constables, metropolitan
and indigenous, had already made their
way.

"And where will you go, sir?" asked the
sergeant of Lund. " Will you knock up
the people at the Mitre Hotel? You must
want rest."

" A newspaper man can do with considerably less rest than a policeman. Besides, I have slept a good deal on the
journey; and, moreover, I should very
much like, if not out of order, to follow
your movements as closely as possible.
May I keep with you? I have an old

friend here to whom I shall go later in the day; but I should like to keep in your company at all events until he is stirring."

" Do so, by all means."

" I really can tell you more about the localities here, especially perhaps your man's likely haunts, than anybody else."

" You are furthering the ends of justice beyond a doubt, sir. Remain with us by all means."

The resources of the Zoar police-station were not of the Sybarite order, but they included some hot coffee with bread-and-butter, and a rinse under the pump; so that, in a quarter of an hour, the exploring party were ready to start, and the sergeant expressed a strong wish to go first of all to the scene of the murder. He could not explain why, but a sort of fascination seemed to lure him thither.

" I don't for one moment imagine we are going to find our man there or thereabouts," he said, "but still I feel as though I should like to go there, and take my bearings from thence."

"From that spot," replied Lund, "you can see his church—the man you want is a parson, you will recollect—and also a new house his father is building hard by."

"Both of them interesting, if not actually important localities. For myself, I confess I have no heart in this matter. The authorities say 'Go to Zoar,' and I go. They say, 'From information we have received, the alleged murderer has been in or near Zoar lately.' On the information so received I act; but to me it seems so unlikely that a man would go and run his head into the very place where suspicion would be hottest against him, and where every blessed soul he met would know him, that it seems actually unreasonable to be looking for him here."

"Still we may get a clue."

"We may, as you say, get a clue. Scent lies very long in murder cases, and one dog may take it up where another fails to do so."

" True."

" And that place is the Bishop's palace, you say? Well, it is a tumbledown old spot; and, as for the water round it, I should say it must be damp. I should have it drained."

" My good fellow, you'll kill me if you go on talking in such a practical way of these dear romantic old spots."

" Well then, I won't: but then I am a practical man, and this spot appears to me more rheumatic than romantic."

" Dreadful! I actually used to think I would dwarf my mind down to the episcopal standard to live and die in such a sequestered spot as that. Five thousand a year and that tumbledown old palace, as you term it, form a terrible temptation to believe that whatever is is best."

" Then the bishops are mostly Conservative, are they ?"

" In reality, yes; though often, when nominees of Liberal Governments, they are bound to be Liberal too in name; but as sure as ever real Liberal principles prevailed, that palace ruin would be put into thorough decorative repair, the moat drained, and even the west front of the cathedral touched up according to the tastes of the nineteenth instead of the thirteenth century."

"Surely we have learned a thing or two in those six hundred years."

"To be consistent, you Protestants should have learned to do without your so-called bishops, who are no more bishops than I am."

"Indeed, sir. Then it seems a good deal of money, if we don't get the real article after all."

"It pertaineth to the office of a bishop—mind, I mean one of your Brummagem Protestant duffer-bishops—to keep things quiet just for his own time, and to let the future take thought for the things of itself. Disestablishment cannot be far off, and they know it; disendowment may follow, and that is all they care about. The old ship is rotten, and vexes the souls of real religious Plimsolls; but all these old ladies want is to tinker up the timbers and keep them afloat, so that they may draw their salaries for the term of their natural lives. I begin to agree with you, sergeant, the old place does want repairing. Come along, it makes me feel more bitterly than I like when I look at it, remembering whose it really is, and how might is the only right of the present possessors."

" And they say you are being kept out of your rights too by this Percy Llewellyn's father. Is that so?"

" Look up there," said Lund, pointing with his walking-stick to the northern heights round Zoar, " you see that new house being built?"

" Yes; I can make out the scaffolding. Is that yours?"

" By right, yes; at least my wife's, which comes to the same thing. There my worthy uncle and the father of the rascal we are hunting up is building himself—or rather building us—a lordly mansion; for we'll have him out of it as soon as he dares to take possession."

" I hope so."

" There can be no doubt of it. My lawyer here has a will in his hands which proves Edward's title invalid."

" If it's a case of lawyer against lawyer you may just as well toss up. You've got just as much chance of coming by your rights."

" You believe in lawyers, it appears to me, just about as much as I do in Brummagem bishops."

" Just about."

The exploring party now quitted the enceinte of the Bishop's palace, and came to the lane skirted by the overhanging woods. How vividly this brought back to Lund's mind the events of his Zoar life, especially the stolen meetings with Elsie, when he won her heart from Percy; most specially of all the night when he parted from the poor murdered girl, and lost her and Percy

Llewellyn in the shadows cast by these same woods. This perpetuity and permanence in Nature strikes us very forcibly when the circumstances of our own lives have greatly changed. We seem to think, unreasonably enough, that Nature should have changed too. Alec wondered whether the apathetic policeman could appreciate this change of scenery.

" Magnificent wood, sergeant, is it not?"

" Wants thinning, sir," was again the practical reply.

" For the sake of timber, yes, perhaps. But looking at it from a professional point of view, as an active and intelligent officer should look, can you picture a better situation for a murder? Try to consider murder as one of the fine arts, and tell me, could you have a better background for your picture?"

"No; it's very good," replied the sergeant, not caring to commit himself to any very decided opinion, "but the murder didn't happen here, because the girl was drowned, and he couldn't have drowned her on a hillside like that."

"No; we are coming to the precise spot by-and-by. I want to tone your mind to a proper condition before leading you to the precise scene of action. Yonder you see, to the left, are the fish-ponds, and beyond them the spire of St. Simon Magus' Church."

"That was his church?"

"Yes. Now at this stile, over which we are going to get in a moment, it was that I first discovered there was anything between Percy and the murdered girl."

"How came that about?"

"We were coming down the lane from the other end, opposite where you and I entered it, and heard Percy and Mary Baker in conversation——"

"You say 'we;' from which I argue you were not alone."

"And rightly so," answered Lund, smiling. "I am not using the word in the royal manner in which it is employed in newspapers."

"Was it a young lady too?"

"Yes; it was my present wife who was with me."

"Ah, that was all on the square," remarked the sergeant, seeming quite relieved to find that the meeting was, as he deemed, a legitimate one.

"Well, scarcely on the square either. My wife was then engaged to Percy Llewellyn."

"And you took her away from him. Now there, you see, is an advantage of my having you here and talking over the matter with you on the spot; it brings the matter life-like before my mind. That question of motive isn't one that could be put into legal shape and used in Court perhaps, but it's one that comes home to our minds, nevertheless."

Then Alec Lund told the group of policemen, for the other two joined them at the stile, the whole trite history of his involuntary eavesdropping when Percy Llewellyn and Mary Baker parted at the stile.

"On the evening when the poor girl came by her death, I met her by appointment here again."

"She made the appointment, did she? It was a strange place to fix upon, considering it was where you caught her before."

"And somewhat spoils your notion about people not going to unlikely places, doesn't it? Do you know, I believe if I had committed that murder I should feel the same sort of fascination they say Eugene Aram did to come back to the scene of it."

"Should you now indeed? I shouldn't. But about Mary Baker. Did your wife know of the appointment?"

"She did. I had vague suspicions of something wrong between Percy and Mary—I forgot to tell you, but perhaps you remember, she was a singer in his church choir.".

"I recollect; that came out at the trial."

"She was a light, silly, vain little doll,

and had half confessed to me. I wanted to get at the whole truth; and, as she would not see my wife, I consented to meet her here."

"Dangerous," moralised the policeman.

"It was; but I never gave that a thought. Percy interrupted us as we were walking on this very path——"

"Hand-in-hand, I have been told."

"Yes; I was coaxing her to tell me the truth. It looked suspicious, of course."

"Fishy, to a degree. Was there a row?"

"Not a bit. He simply took her away. She even rounded on me, as you would say; declared I had asked her to take a walk, and promised in my presence that she would never walk out with me or anybody else any more, but would go home to her mother and be a good girl."

"Did she now? Well, that was artful. She was a milliner, was she not?"

"Yes; I never could understand why

that particular line of business should so
often make girls turn out ill."

"It's the dress. From dressing other
folks, they take to decorating themselves.
That makes the young fellows take notice
of them; and they are but poor vain
creatures after all. Now when they left
you which way did they go?"

"Down the lane by which we came this
morning."

"And you?"

"Not to appear to follow them, I went
in the opposite direction past the Church
yonder and down the main street of East
Zoar."

"Then to get to the pond, they must
have turned directly on their heels and
retraced their steps?"

"Yes."

"Let's just walk over the course, and try
it. They must have come back here to the
stile—we will suppose they came so far—
and then struck across to the pond. Let's
trespass on this fine meadow-land so as to

do it. I wonder whether it occurred to your police here to look for footsteps across the field?"

"I fancy the grass got so trodden before the body was found, that all traces would be obliterated."

"What made them think of looking in the pond?"

"Only because they had exhausted all other places. Besides Llewellyn, of course, told them he had left the girl with me here in this field. It was part of his devilish scheme."

"A good plant in truth."

"Yes; I forgot—that is your word."

"Supposing them to have got to the brink of the pond, the theory is that a struggle took place."

"There were evident marks of it here. I cannot imagine under what pretext he could have got the poor girl to the edge of the water."

Dismissing this difficulty as irrelevant to the inquiry, the sergeant took stock of all

the surroundings, and looked at Alec Lund
very much as though he meant to make the
experiment of capsizing him into the deep,
dark water below.

"Now show me as near as you can,
young mister, where this glove of yours was
found."

"Here, I believe, some six or seven yards
from where the struggle took place."

"What a beautiful bit of evidence," said
the sergeant, with the air of a connoisseur.
"Shouldn't I have kept my eye on you, as
the saying goes?"

"No doubt they did."

"Very likely not. They have a free-and-
easy way of doing things down in the
country here which doesn't suit us London
officials. Now about the depth of this
water. Lend us your stick, sir, will you?"

The sergeant commenced his soundings,
and the other two men sauntered quietly
along the bank speculating on the stock of
fish in the pond. Alec was lost in admira-
tion of the cathedral, from which the

morning mists had now cleared away, and it stood out bold and distinct in the morning sunlight. Next to the west front this was generally considered to be one of the finest views. He tried once more to interest his companion in the noble old edifice, but to no purpose. At the imminent risk of falling into the water he was hanging on to a bush on the bank, and poking away at the pond with the walking-stick he had borrowed.

"Have you fished up anything very important, or are you only bent on discovering to the very eighth of an inch the depth of the mud deposit?"

The sergeant made no reply at first, but went on prodding so very vigorously that Alec was fain to come up to the pond and see what he was about. Then the man, mad with excitement, towed something along with the handle of the stick, and forgot his official dignity so far as to swear.

"D—me if I haven't got him!"

"Who?"

"Llewellyn. Look here."

And, surely enough, floating on the surface of the muddy water, and towed along by the crook of Alec Lund's stick was the dead body of Percy Llewellyn; the pale face looking placidly up from the dirty pond, like a common-place reproduction of the Christian Martyr.

Lured by some strange fascination he had come to kill himself in the very place where he had sacrificed his victim so long ago.

"Didn't I tell you we should find something here?" said the sergeant, immediately, after the manner of his craft, appropriating all the honour and glory to himself, and looking down upon his treasure-trove with an air of supreme satisfaction. "Call those men, and let's get the body out."

"As far as I can recollect, you said it was useless looking for Llewellyn in Zoar, that it wasn't likely he'd come here of all places in the world, and scouted my idea of his feeling any attraction to this particular spot."

"Never you mind. Call the fellows. It will be work enough for the four of us to get him up. He is as heavy as lead."

By the united efforts of the men the body was at length drawn from the water and deposited, a dank, limp mass on the grass, as nearly as possible in the same spot where, but a short time before, the poor girl had been laid. It was a consummate piece of retributive justice. Vengeance seemed satisfied in every nicest detail. It was literally an eye for an eye and a tooth for a tooth that the presumptive murderer had rendered in expiation of his misdeeds. Perhaps it is always so. Perhaps, if not here, still in a future state, the very uttermost farthing shall be paid for every one of those pleasant sins to which men yield themselves up here; and the payment shall be made in the very coinage wherein the damning debt was contracted. Here the payment curiously forestalled the perfect reprisals of the judgment-day.

When Alec Lund saw his former rival

and foe lying helplessly there, he felt that
thrill of sorrow to which masculine minds
are always liable—often in direct proportion
to their manliness. The man had wrought
him cruel wrong; but he was lying there
done to death no doubt by his own act. A
great big lump swelled up in Alec's throat,
and something very like moisture suffused
his eyes for a moment; but it was only for a
moment. The sergeant saw it, and really
thought his eyes must have deceived him.
He seemed to expect Lund would execute a
war-dance around his prostrate enemy, or
spurn his corpse with his foot.

"Now then, men, off as quick as you
can to the police-station for the stretcher;"
and the men prepared to obey with alacrity.
"Keep all quiet; and Mr. Lund and myself
will remain on guard here. You don't look
as pleased as I could have expected, sir."

"It's a sickening sight; and, though I
am pretty well case-hardened like yourself,
family considerations come in to complicate
my feelings in this particular case. This

man, remember, was to have married the lady who is now my wife."

"Then you'll pardon me for saying that, under the circumstances, I should think this is about the best place for him."

"On all hands—except so far as it adds another sin to his account—this is perhaps the best end that could have come to the unfortunate man. Public punishment would have been terrible for all his family."

"And he most certainly would have swung. Well, there's an old saying, that the man who is born to be hung won't drown. I suppose the reverse is true, too."

While the sergeant thus moralized, and speculated upon the verdict of the inevitable coroner's inquest, Alec studied minutely the features of the dead man as they lay there, upturned to the clear blue sky. Percy had aged considerably; and, though the refining influence of death had its usual effect of softening down some harsh lines, there were signs on the countenance that the dead man's recent existence—now closed so abruptly—had been a degrading one. It had never been a pleasing, though withal somewhat of a handsome face. Now, in addition to the disfigurements of the water, there were marks upon it like those of the jail-bird, which will supervene even upon the most refined visage sometimes after a very short incarceration and association with convicts. The human countenance is plastic, and death throws into bold relief the prominent characteristics of life. It harmonises them; but the result is not always pleasing. Do we not seem to discern in this circumstance an index to the fact that in the after-world, while the good have greater scope for their goodness, the bad shall have proportionately larger facilities for evil?

Anon the men returned with some of their local confrères, followed by that small knot of tagrag and bobtail which seems to lurk in ambush for every movement of the police stretcher. Generally it was nothing more than a rustic debauchee, who was brought home with the milk, after making a night of it; but now it was another murder, or something equally dreadful. Zoar was getting quite sensational; and the Fishponds formed the very focus of its romance. As they bore away their horrible burthen, Alec could not help glancing once more at the house on Topaz Farm, where, no doubt, the workmen were beginning their labours for the day. As he did so, he asked himself in an audible voice :—

" What will his father say ?"

" Yes," said the sergeant, in his most practical tone, " it will be a nuisance for his family, but better, after all, as we agreed, than an execution outside the county jail."

" I think, considering how nearly that was my fate, you might make fewer allusions to such an issue, sergeant."

" I beg your pardon, I'm sure——"

" I meant nothing," replied Alec. " I wonder," he continued, " whether the dead man has left any statement."

"While you were wool-gathering I took the opportunity of turning out his pockets. I found this small sum of money, his watch—stopped at midnight, I presume—at all events twelve o'clock—and just this scrap of paper addressed to nobody in particular."

"'Vide Dovecot.'"

"Do you know—of course you do—what 'vide' means?" asked the officer.

"'Vide' means 'see!'"

"And Dovecot?"

"Ah, there you bother me," answered Alec Lund. He felt that the paper was meant for him—almost as if the dead man were speaking to him. True—Dovecot Hill was a well-known locality; but Percy had got to learn latterly the secret of the stolen meetings in the nest on Dovecot Hill. Elsie purposely twitted him with it when he had once found it out, and that made Alec quite certain that the address was meant for him. He jumped instinctively to the conclusion that the dead man had made some statement and deposited it in the nest on Dovecot Hill. He was eager to get clear of the police and to go and search on his own account.

"See Dovecot," repeated the sergeant. "Dovecot is the name of a person or a place, no doubt."

"Dovecot Hill is the name of the hill you see opposite, but what can be the meaning of telling us to see that?"

"What indeed?" replied the sergeant, scratching his head and twisting the scrap of paper every way as if to make it mean something more than it really did.

"I should advise you to take a constitutional, sergeant, and examine every nook and cranny of Dovecot Hill. You have been so lucky this morning that you are sure to find something."

"Ah, now you are chaffing me. No, it can't mean that. It must be some house, or some person. Is there no house, no person of that name?"

"None."

"You are sure?"

"I know every inch of this place; and am on speaking terms with nearly everybody, except the infants in arms—who, of course, can't speak."

"Then it beats me; but it also reminds me that some one ought to go and tell his family. It would not be decent to let his father go to business as though nothing had happened."

"By no means."

"Will you undertake the unpleasant duty of breaking it to him, Mr. Lund?" asked the sergeant.

"Certainly not. You had better do it in your official capacity. I have no reason to treat my uncle with consideration. The son is dead, and beyond my wrath, but I make no terms with the father. He is reaping the whirlwind, but he sowed the storm himself."

"Direct me to the house, and I will go at once."

"I will take you halfway there myself."

"Where are you going?"

"To call on my friend the Precentor, who lives in the Vicar's Close; he will be up by this time."

So off they set together, and met a long procession of sensation-mongers coming out to see the scene of what they now knew to be a suicide.

Briggs was just sitting serenely down to his modest breakfast in his little mediævally-adorned room, and Alec's arrival quite dissipated all ideas of quietude for the day. It was very questionable whether Briggs was glad or sorry at the interruption. Quiet people get into such a groove that the slightest deviation from it becomes in a degree painful. However he soon got interested in Alec's story; and it was agreed that after he had supplemented the rude repast and imperfect ablutions of the early morning with the resources of Briggs's larder and dressing-case, Alec should go and call on the Dean.

"Then," he said; "after service, I want you to take a walk with me, Briggs."

"With pleasure. Anywhere in particular?"

"Yes; Dovecot Hill."

"For what purpose?"

"'Vide Dovecot.'"

"I thought you told the policeman you didn't understand that."

"So I did, but I didn't tell you so."

"Do you understand it?"

"Perfectly."

"What does it mean?"

"I may be wrong. Do you mind waiting for the result? Will you walk with me first, and let me tell you afterwards?"

"Certainly."

The Dean was glad to see his young friend again; and as for Mrs. Dean, her anxiety about Elsie—and especially about Elsie's baby—was intense. Never having had any babies herself, she had not entertained the idea that Elsie would ever commit herself in that way. She was disappointed that Alec's knowledge of his son

and heir seemed so imperfect. He was
abstracted and lowspirited, and much more
inclined to talk to the Dean than to his
wife, which, by the way had not been the
case in former days, when Alec leaned
rather to conversation with the lady. The
Dean had a habit of larding his everyday
discourse with fragments of Aristotle, or
letting off little classical popguns in the
shape of quotations from the Greek Tragedians; and this bored him exceedingly.

"I am going to take Lund for a long
walk after service, and see if I cannot raise
his spirits, sir," said Briggs.

"Do. Take him for a spurt up Dovecot
Hill."

"The very place we had arranged. It's
an old haunt of Lund's."

"Oh yes, we know all about it, do we
not, Mr. Lund, in old times? Elsie could
tell us some stories about that. I tremble
for the morals of that poor infant."

"Surely it can't be wrong to flirt with
your wife."

"But she wasn't your wife then, she was——" and the old lady hesitated.

"I know what you are going to say; she was nearly the wife of Percy Llewellyn—the dead man I saw drawn from his un-hallowed grave to-day. I often wonder whether it would not have been better had I never come to complicate the arrange-ments of this excellent family."

"Lund," returned the Dean, with great solemnity, "do you for one moment hint that you would have allowed—or rather that you now wish you had allowed, Elsie to link her fate with that libertine?"

"But it was I who was the libertine then, at least who had the character of being one. I never could quite make out why."

"Thank your stars, Mr. Lund," said the Dean's wife, following out her husband's train of thought, "that it was your good fortune to get Elsie. Be a good husband to her, and above all, take care of the son and heir."

"The bells are just striking out for morning prayer, Alec," continued the Dean. "I wish I could sing the service, I would let Briggs off to take you for a walk at once. And I wish one thing still more."

"What is that?"

"That your change of creed did not prevent you from worshipping with us in the old place."

"Prevent me!"

"Don't you think us all heretics?"

"I am not quite so far gone as that, my dear Dean; and just at this moment I know nothing I should enjoy so much as renewing old associations by going to cathedral."

"Come then. I say, Briggs," the old dignitary added, with a smile, "there are hopes of this dear boy yet; and to you, as Locum Tenens of St. Simon Magus—now vacant, by the way—I entrust the task of converting him. Lund is very, very far too good a fellow to let slip."

After service the two friends set out together for Dovecot Hill; and Alec Lund took the earliest opportunity when they were alone, of congratulating Briggs on the evident intention of the Dean to suggest his appointment to the incumbency of St. Simon Magus.

"I don't know, my dear fellow," answered the modest little Precentor, "whether it would be such a subject for congratulation, even if true, which I very much doubt."

"No cause for congratulation! Why not?"

"As incumbent of St. Simon Magus I should have to do lots of things inconsistent with my present state of repose; amongst others to——"

"What?"

"Marry. I can see a bachelor incumbent is a mistake."

"And are there not dozens of nice girls in the Zoar horse-boxes at every service? Marry one of these, and be happy."

Briggs didn't see it; and preferred to

talk of something else. The difficulty of mounting the steep side of Dovecot Hill suspended all conversation for the moment.

When they arrived at the summit Alec Lund made at once for his old nest among the limestone rocks. There it was as cosy as ever, recalling vividly his first and many subsequent meetings with Elsie. It was clear, however, the place had been recently occupied. The grass was trodden down, and there was a kind of pillow made from fresh fern at one end. Behind this pillow there was a projection of the rock, forming quite a little cavern below. Here he had often secreted his book in olden days when he planned a visit on the morrow and was too lazy to carry the volume home. The projection made the place quite inaccessible to rain, and by pushing the book well under, it was rendered quite invisible from without. Alec Lund went to this receptacle as if by instinct, put his arm well under, and from the further extremity drew forth a manuscript book.

"I thought so," he said, showing Briggs his prize.

" What is it ?"

"A volume in Llewellyn's handwriting, entitled, 'A Murderer's Journal.' Let us sit down and read it here."

So they sat in the old familiar nest, and read the characters recently traced by the hand that was now cold and rigid in death.

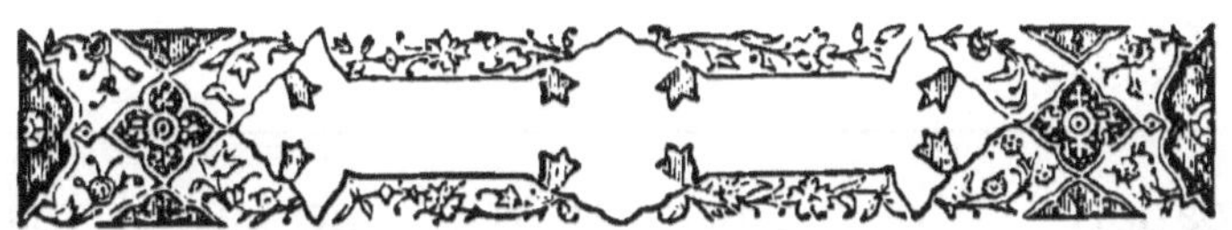

CHAPTER III.

UNARTISTIC as it must of necessity appear, should this journal ever come to form part of the family story, which I more than suspect Elsie to be writing or compiling, I still desire to put it at once on record in the very forefront, that I am guilty of the murder of Mary Baker. No hand but mine did that black deed. How and why I did it, and how far I have expiated my crime by subsequent suffering, it will be the purpose of this journal to show. I may be arrested at any moment; if I am, I shall at once plead guilty; I have made up my mind to that. But, before such a contingency occurs, I desire, purely for my own comparative peace of mind, to put this confession on

paper. When I used to read the narratives
of murderers, and saw how they seemed to
feel a satisfaction in writing down the
details of their crimes, it always appeared to
me so curious a psychological problem that
I could not understand or solve it. I
comprehend it thoroughly now. Every
such detail forming, as it were, a separate
clause in the confession, serves to lighten
the load of guilt—seems to ease the bosom
of one more black secret which it longs to
disgorge.

"I do not address anybody in particular,
because I cannot guess under what circumstances this confession will be made
public; nor do I much care. If my fate
comes to suicide, as it most probably will,
it is very likely I shall make Lund the
depositary of my confession; not out of
regard to him, I have not one particle of
what is nicknamed Christian feeling towards
him: I hate him; and even now regret
that the trial did not go against him, for I
still consider him indirectly the cause of

Mary Baker's murder. If he had not come to Zoar and interrupted all our family arrangements, it would never have occurred."

"Pleasant for me," was the comment of Alec Lund, as he read the narrative aloud to his friend Briggs.

"Very. But read on. I am terribly interested in this strange story."

"I don't know that I ever loved my cousin Elsie particularly, and I am quite sure that she did not love me—latterly at all events; but probably the conditions under which we should have come together were as good as those which exist in nine out of ten marriages. People don't marry for love in these times; it's bad form, and looks like straining after old romantic Corydon and Phyllis days. Perhaps I can carry my mind back to a time when some such idyllic notions had a transient resting-place in my brain or heart, as they say; but it was when I was quite a boy. I don't think Elsie was as bad as I was at the time, though we talked a good deal of

nonsense, half of which I am rejoiced to
have forgotten. I hope, if there be any
hereafter, which I have happily begun to
doubt, we may forget all the nonsense of
this exceedingly ridiculous mundane existence. You see, whoever you are that
happens to read this narrative, whether jail
chaplain or Alexander Lund, I am quite
cynical, and not at all in what my reverend
brothers would term a proper frame of mind.

"And here again I would say a word on
my so-called religious opinions, though I
really do not know that they concern anybody but myself. I own no sort of right
on the part of another person to catechise
me as to my creed or practice. I take the
risk on myself, and am now standing on
the very frontier-line of that state where I
had so long taught others, as almost myself,
to believe that we should reap the rewards
or incur the punishment of the deeds done
in the body. It may be so yet. I am
now, however, acutely conscious that I was
a hypocrite in teaching this, and therefore

a hypocrite also in all my clerical ministrations at Zoar. I am not in the least sorry for this. I am not going to write one word in the Uriah Heap or interesting penitent style; but I think it was a mistake. I should have done better to stick to the law; my father made a mistake when he urged me to combine the Gospel. My father, I may observe in passing, has none of the elements of a successful schemer in him. He has all the will, but none of the ability. Sam is transcendent in that respect. The way in which he and Patty blend sixty per cent. with Evangelical religion is incomparable. I blush to think of the bungling way in which Llewellyn and Son managed the Topaz Farm business. If Lund had not been a besotted fool, he would have ousted everybody the day after he married Elsie. I would."

"That's a confirmation of your view of the case, Lund," said Briggs.

"It was too patent to need confirmation," he replied, and then continued reading :—

" Perhaps it is an unconscious effort of mine to patch up matters before I make my exit from this terrestrial sphere, but I have a great notion that I am not different from other clerics in this respect. I believe if you could sound the not very abysmal depths of that insignificant Precentor who, I find, is put in to keep St. Simon Magus' warm, you would discover that the only thing true about him was his mild tenor voice. He believes no more than I did, and only acts because it pays. If another Mary Baker came in his way under the embarrassing circumstances with which my Mary Baker was surrounded, he would in his turn present the example of 'another good man gone wrong'—as the little boys say.

" After the most rigid self-analysis, I am puzzled quite to account for my attitude towards that girl. To suppose that I who plead guilty to never having loved the woman destined to be my wife, could have fallen in love with such a doll-faced chit as that, would be preposterous. Even passion would be too strong a term to use in this case. What was it, then? Sometimes I am half disposed to believe in succubi— tricksy spirits sent in the form of pretty girls to play the dickens with strong men's common-sense. I never 'spooned' with my cousin Elsie after the date of the bread-and-butter age, though she was comely enough in all respects, and her intellectual acquirements rendered her a thorough companion for a man: but I did waste my sweetness on this pretty doll, who could not say ten words without murdering the Queen's English. How enigmatical is this ridiculously complicated physical and intellectual constitution of ours! On the supposition that these low spirits are incarnated for man's special obfuscation, the process becomes somewhat plainer, though still obscure. I was prodigiously ashamed of myself, I recollect, when I found that Elsie had witnessed our love-making one evening at the stile by the Fishponds field—not because it was likely to injure my reputation, or to make her jealous, but because it seemed so utterly silly on my part.

"Of course there could be but one end to such a connexion as this. Into that particular I decline to go further than to leave on record a protest against imputing all the crime to a man in these cases. It seems cowardly perhaps to write against a girl whom you have first 'wronged'—as the cant phrase goes—and then murdered; but recollect, if you please, that, before this document is read, death will have equalized us in this respect. If I commit suicide, I shall only let its whereabouts be divulged by something found on my body. If I am executed, I shall make a stipulation that my last dying speech and confession be not made public until after that interesting event. They always preserve the strictest faith with condemned criminals in these matters; much more punctiliously than they do with respectable people who have made the mistake of failing in life."

" Llewellyn evidently had a notion," said Alec, in the brief pause occasioned by a turn in the MS., "that the kingdom of Heaven was specially designed for those who had failed on earth."

"Proceed."

"Passing over this unsavoury phase of the subject, then, in which I maintain I was not the aggressor, I come to a time when its results were beginning to appear, amongst other ways in the shape of taunts from Mary to myself as to my hypocrisy, and still more, in threats of exposure if I did not marry her. All this time, recollect, the girl was singing in my choir, and, whenever I said a more than usually telling thing in church, and saw all the old ladies looking up to me as a demigod, I was conscious of that lynx-eye in the west gallery on a level with my own in the pulpit, looking threateningly at me for the very unction which I so laboriously threw into my pulpit utterances. This was the sort of purgatory into which I had got myself by my faux pas.

"Her mother, she said, she felt certain guessed the true state of things. Look at my own aunts, they had ceased to come to my church. No doubt 'mother' had told them. Could I not see the wisdom of marrying her, if only by way of making a virtue of necessity. Let us be married and go to some country living, as I had intended to do if I had married 'Miss Elsie.' We could be so happy. The murderous fit always came over me when she took this tone. I could bear her taunts and abuse far better than her affection. I suppose I must use that term advisedly. I suppose she did love me; only I do not think I quite understand what people mean when they talk of love. Of course, the girlish, young-ladyish idea of the thing is quite out of the question.

"Into this complication I was led, mark you (whoever you may be), by Lund's having disarranged our family plans. I felt a sense of vacancy when Elsie utterly gave me up at last, and I vowed to be revenged if I could, though I never thought destiny would place in my hands such a splendid opportunity as actually occurred. I hope still to gratify that revenge, if one really does survive the extinction of the organism. If I can 'haunt' you, Lund, I will."

And Alec, as he read, looked round as if half expecting to see some airy shape by his side. He saw nothing as yet, however, and went on reading.

"I come now to the time when my revered parent's anxiety to shut up the High Street shop, and to establish himself as a quasi-squire at Topaz, brought Lund and Elsie on the scene at Zoar again. The espousal of Elsie's cause by the Dean was more than my father could bear, and even Sam was non-plussed at the turn things had taken. Lund had gone to Doctors' Commons and found the true state of the Topaz title by unearthing Susanna Dash's will. How Morris Llewellyn's could ever have been drawn by any but lunatics, while that other interesting testamentary docu-ment was in existence, I am at a loss to

imagine. I was but a youngster, and did
not feel so strongly on the subject of £ s. d.
as I afterwards got to. As to 'position' I
did not care a straw. That was the rock on
which my infatuated parents split. When
once I was in the Church and beneficed, I
took my revenge by adopting an Evangelical
tone in opposition to the mild Puseyism
prevalent in Zoar. I own now, though
it seems 'small' to say it, I should have
liked, as well as my parents, to be in
cathedral society at Zoar. But I saw this
was impossible since Elsie had given me
the go-by, so I revenged myself, not very
successfully, I fear, in the way I have
mentioned.

"There was some vague notion, I recollect, on our parts that, if we could get
Lund to the governor's office, we might
make him commit himself in some way, or
sign something or other to his own preju-
dice. Sam, who was always lying in ambush
for somebody in his own business, was to
hide in the strong room and catch Lund

tripping if possible. Any such scheme as this was spoilt by my father getting in a rage with Lund about Aunt Phillis's will being in Sheppard's hands. The circumstance of the Dean and young Briggs being brought in as witnesses on Lund's side too, did not mend matters; and all that was got out of that visit was by me. Lund dropped his glove, which the clerk put on the governor's table, and I pocketed, thinking it might one day come in useful. This I did on Sam's advice. 'Whenever you can grab anything of anybody else's,' said this nine-teenth century saint, 'do it my boy. You never know when it may come useful.' My treasure-trove came in useful very soon.

"I have no notion what took me to the Fishponds field on the evening in question. It is true I once used to walk there in order to meet Mary, even when we had no assignation, but that represented a much earlier era in our love-making. It was natural for me to walk in that direction as my church was there, and if anybody saw us together they thought nothing of it, as they fancied, of course, we were going to St. Simon's. Nothing of the kind, however, led me in that direction then, I am sure; but I felt an uncontrollable desire to walk to the Fishponds. In the absence of other explanation, I must consider that the deed had to be done, and I was sent thither to do it. Anyhow I went, and found Alexander Lund walking with Mary Baker. I suppose I felt angry; for I distinctly recollect congratulating myself on having the glove in my pocket. Yes; if malice aforethought be necessary to constitute murder, I am afraid I murdered Mary Baker very much indeed.

" Not but what, even then, I believe, if anybody had said to me in so many words, ' You will kill that girl and throw the glove down beside where you murdered her, so as to implicate Lund,' I should have scarcely been equal to it. Our tempters, whoever they are, manage matters with more finesse than this. I wonder whether there is any truth in demoniacal possession. I begin to think there were symptoms of a second personality about my actions that night.

"As soon as Lund and I had got our quarrel over, and he had gone on his way towards St. Simon Magus', we turned towards the wood, and she asked me with a shrill, almost hysterical laugh—

"'Is it possible you are jealous of that fellow Lund?'"

"That was the laugh you heard, Alec." said Briggs.

"Yes."

"'Jealous or not jealous,' I replied (Alec continued to read), 'I will take care you never give me cause for jealousy again.'

"'How so?' she asked, defiantly; 'what will you do, pray?'

"'Do! Tell your mother, and have you locked in your room, or sent out of the place altogether.'

"'Fancy mother locking *me* in *my* room!

I'm much more likely to lock her in hers. Besides——'

" ' Besides what ?'

" ' If you can tell her something, I can tell her something, too; and if you or I don't tell her, Lund will.'

" ' How does he know it ?'

" ' I told him myself.'

" ' If I thought you really had, you deceitful little minx, do you know what I would do ?'

" ' What ?'

" ' Hurl you down into that water, as sure as there is a God in heaven.'

" ' Oh don't, Percy; let's come away. It looks so black and horrible.'

" ' Lest I should be too much tempted, you mean, eh ? On second thoughts I won't come away. I'll stand here by the very brink, and make you swear you haven't told him.'

" ' I can't swear that, because I have; and if it comes to that, you know people must be told, and very quickly too——'

" ' How so ?'

" ' How so ? You must marry me, and at once. If not——'

" The temptation *was* too strong. She went in and sank—I remember the quotation rushing through my mind—like lead in the mighty waters. They talked of a struggle on the brink. There was very little. She certainly did try once or twice to lure me from the place ; but at the last there was no struggle at all. I threw her in as though she had been a child, and she never screamed or even came to the surface. I stopped there expecting she would, and determined to force her in again if she got to the bank. Nothing but her death would have satisfied me then.

" People talk of the horror which seizes a man when he finds he has taken a life. There is not the slightest reason why I should indulge in bravado now ; indeed, I wish I could say I was sorry for what I had done. What I am trying to do is to write down impartially my own feelings. I was not sorry. I felt as though a load were off my mind now Mary was dead; but I also felt the instinct of self-preservation excessively strong upon me. I must turn suspicion from myself to somebody else. Then I thought of the glove again. I could not possibly doubt that Fate had arranged that beautiful bit of circumstantial evidence for me. Lund had been walking with the girl in the Fishponds field by daylight; it was dark when I surprised them. Somebody must have seen them. I therefore trod heavily about the bank, and tore the grass and shrubs a little, to make it appear that there had been a struggle, as I thought that would look more natural. Then I cleaned my boots and clothes of every speck of mud, dropped the glove, went home and spent the evening serenely in the bosom of my family.

"I waited quite anxiously for the messenger to come from Mrs. Baker, asking me if I knew anything of her daughter. It was not the anxiety of fear; quite the con-

trary. I felt that the first step we made in
that search, was like winding the first mesh
of a coil round Alec Lund."

" Pleasant young gentleman, that relative
of yours, Alec," was Briggs's comment.

" The widow kept early hours, so I had
not long to wait. We were just taking our
negus, previous to going upstairs, when the
expected summons came. My mother,
when she heard what it was all about
(which was some considerable time, on
account of her deafness), protested warmly.
against my going out at that time of night
to look after a loose girl, who was no
doubt skylarking somewhere or other; but
I objected to any such assumption in a
tone of virtuous indignation, and assured
the widow I would not rest until I had
found her daughter. I advised her to go
round to the police-station, saying, I would
meet her there with Mr. Moddle in as short
a time as possible.

" I did not confess to Moddle, principally
because I felt it might be embarrassing to

him; but I think Moddle knew. He stared as if he had seen Mary Baker's ghost when I told him what had happened; and I am quite sure he would not have been a safe man to be entrusted with the secret. He guessed it, I think, though he did not say so; but he did no more, and off we set together to help the police search for the body.

"Of course I told them all I knew, or rather all it suited my purpose to pretend to know, of what took place on the evening of the murder.

"This came out at the trial, so I need not go over it again. The Fishpond is a good big place, so I did not pounce down upon the right spot at once; and hunting in the dead of night is slow work. When they got to the right place, and discovery was inevitable, I lagged behind a little, and let the police find the glove. They pocketed it mysteriously at first, so as not to lose any of the fame and honour attaching to the discovery, and then they found out the marks I had made the night before as symptoms of a terrible struggle. The torn shrubs pointed to the spot in the pond where the actual drowning had taken place; but the depth here was quite fathomless by any ordinary implements, such as sticks and umbrellas. Boat-hooks and drags had to be got, and all this took a long time in Zoar; so that it was broad daylight when we found the body and took it home. I closed the eyes myself, and had a queer notion that they stared at me significantly when I did so. The mother seemed to notice this too."

"We know she did, Briggs, as I told you."

" Yes."

" Over the particulars of Lund's trial and acquittal I need not take my readers. I put it thus in the plural because I quite hope Elsie will utilise this narrative as a chapter in the family romance. I little thought when she began that silly story, that I should be the means of contributing so interesting an incident to it.

"I bolted when Lund was found not guilty, just for the sake of gaining time. It came out so clearly that he or I must have done the deed, that, after his acquittal, I knew my arrest and conviction must be only matters of time. I suppose I am—or at all events I was then—as tenacious of life as most people. I would not, however, make the mistake of trying to get out of England, as I was certain the ports would be watched; so I sped Londonwards, stopping short at a suburban station in case I might be expected at the terminus; and, after that date, my movements were really determined by the announcements I saw in the daily papers. The freedom of the press is a glorious privilege for Englishmen, especially when they have committed a murder, or in any other way broken the law. The public are so very exacting in their demands to know all about a suspected criminal, and the police system of England is so notoriously defective, that energetic reporters can get anything they want out of our active and intelligent officers. I put it on record here, for the benefit of the force and the discomfiture of future homicides, that I changed my place of residence from time to time entirely on the suggestion of the newspaper reports.

" During all this time, I still assert as a nut for psychologists to crack, that I never felt the slightest horror on account of what I had done *per se.* I simply saw that it had been a disagreeable necessity which would one day cost me my life, but as to doubting that, were the thing to be done over again, I should do it, I never felt this, nor do I feel it now—I mean at the date of writing. What may be the case when this comes to be read, of course I cannot say.

" The knowledge I thus formed of suburban London was extensive ; and, had it been acquired under other circumstances, would have been interesting. I am decidedly of opinion that there is no such place for anybody who is ' wanted ' as the outskirts of a great city. In the streets of the city itself he would be likely to run against acquaintances, but at Dalston, Gunnersbury, or Brixton, the chances of collision are very remote. At one and all I gave myself out as a student who had retired from the circle of his friends to coach for an examination, so that my landladies were not scandalised by the fact of my having no letters and never going out until after dark. I was obliged to confide my whereabouts to Moddle through whom the governor sent supplies, but only of my own money. He would not give me a sou, for he felt that I had compromised the family, not by my crime, but by being found out, and so dashing to earth for ever his hopes of dining with the Bishop or Dean. Considering what a wretched old bungler he has been, and the dead certainty there is of his coming to grief, perhaps even before I do, his anathemas against myself are very rich indeed. My one mistake has been confiding in Moddle. If it had not been for that I should have been safe for

ever, I believe. Sam would have been
safer, and would have undertaken the
business of sending me supplies—for a
consideration. Sam would do anything for
a consideration.''

" You see I am getting my verdict as to
the various members of the Llewellyn
family confirmed very satisfactorily," said
Alec.

" Would you kindly read your narrative
and give me your comments by way of
appendix ?   What was that ?"

" What ?"

" I thought I saw a shadow fall in front
of us exactly like that of a human being."

" Percy's ghost, no doubt. Nonsense,
man, it was only a passing cloud. I've
spent days upon days here without seeing a
person. It's as safe as Percy's suburban
residences."

" Well, go on."

" By degrees I got bolder and ventured
into town at night occasionally. I also got
to feel sometimes—not horror ; no, I still

protest against that—but I felt like a hunted animal and so got tired of life. One night I felt I must go and give myself up at Bow Street. There Fate stood by me again. Alec Lund was in the doorway, and I would not do it in his presence. He was thrown off his guard for a moment and did not denounce me, but he was after me like a shot, and so were the police. I was too quick for them, however, and got back to the Crab Tree Inn, Fulham, all safe and sound.

"I had fixed my abode here avowedly for aquatic purposes, because I found the sedentary life of a student telling upon my health. I had just begun to realise the possibility of feeling nervous. That was a signal for me to make a complete change, so I have come hither, which is the scene of my writing this present narrative. I manage to get out in a boat for several hours daily, and only read the very lightest of literature in the interim. I am now supposed to be a jolly young waterman,

come down to learn all the twists and turns
of the river ; and I am thus the object of
much observation, though not of the sort I
dread. The first time I dip my sculls in
the water, however, I quite dissipate all
ideas as to my being an expert oarsman.
Only one or two of the most 'cute have
been known to suggest that my bad rowing
is a 'plant'—by which they mean that it is
assumed in order to throw them off their
guard.

"I saw the end coming before that ass
Moddle betrayed my whereabouts. I knew
it could not go on like this. I even felt I
did not want it to go on. As long as I die
game, I do not care how soon I have to
write 'Vixi.'

"*Shall* I die game? The question has
been forced in upon me disagreeably. I
wrote just now in the present tense, I know,
as to not feeling horror; but present and
past tenses are beginning to be jumbled up
in a very peculiar way with me. I try to
persuade myself that the present tense may

still stand in that assertion; but I have promised to write down exactly what I think, and I will do it, though I feel contemptible—ay, yes, *because* I feel contemptible—in doing it. I have had the advent of the horror announced to me since I wrote the above. Excitement has kept me up hitherto. When that fails, the horror will come, and I must die, either by my own or another's hand.

"The night before Moddle betrayed my secret—for I made him confess he *had* betrayed me—I was lying awake in the deep dead night. That is the only time I dread, just about three o'clock in the morning, when all is so awfully still. At the Crab Tree one only hears the sound of the water gliding by, and the melancholy sough of the wind in the trees which stand above the solitary inn. On that particular night, however, which was rather a blustrous one, I heard, as distinctly as ever I heard anything in my life, quite above the sighing of the wind, and apart from the swirl of the water, my own name pronounced by a woman's voice. It was Mary Baker's. If ever she spoke, it was then. I could even detect the faint west-country accent in it, that, once heard, can never be forgotten. I only heard it once. I clutched the match-box, lighted both candles, and kept them burning until broad daylight, when I fell asleep. That was the advent of the horror. I suppose it *is* inevitable after all. I am beginning to think that it is an awful thing to take a fellow-creature's life, even so light and silly a fellow-creature as little Mary—I begin to think of her more tenderly now, always as 'little' Mary. Pshaw! this is maudlin. I have suffered from my want of sleep last night.

"Whilst I am meditating thus, a sharp knock comes at the door of the little parlour where I am breakfasting, or making believe to breakfast; and I am surprised to find my forehead bursting out in great drops of cold perspiration, as I say—

"'Come in.'

"It was Moddle—only Moddle. 'I am so glad to see you, Moddle,' I exclaimed, and saw my visitor look at me inquiringly; for I am not given to be demonstrative.

"'What's the matter?' he asked; 'you seem excited.'

"'Excited! Oh no, Moddle, never more serene in my life.' I was determined he should not know about the horror, at all events.

"'Well, then, I am excited,' he said, 'if you are not. There is no time to waste words. You must cut and run. I fear I have inadvertently betrayed your hiding-place.'

"'The devil you have! To whom?'

"'To those who may tell Lund. Never mind more. Ring the bell, pay your score, and let us be off. I will tell you particulars afterwards.'

"I rang and told the landlord I was an Oxford student, and my tutor had discovered my whereabouts, insisting on my return to the University. How was he to know that college tutors were not in the habit of looking up aquatic young undergrads at the Crab Tree Inn, and bearing them back triumphantly to Alma Mater?

"We drove to the nearest station of the Underground Rail, and by judiciously running to and fro in the bowels of the earth, contrived to throw off the scent anybody who might have been following us. We even parted in the tunnels, and I went home to a new lodging at Kensal Green. There I gave myself out as a recent widower . come to pass a few days near the cemetery where my late wife was buried, which accounted for my sitting nearly all the day among the silent tombs, and made my landlady and her female friends look on me as a model young widower indeed.

"Here, however, I know not whether it was from the nearer presence of the dead lying around me, or from what cause, the horror came again. Whenever I went among those flower-decked graves I heard that gentle voice, not sorrowful as it came to me amid the soughing of the wind and the roll of the distant river in the little inn, but gently and peacefully and—I could not help thinking—with a tone of forgiveness in it, as though it should say, 'Percy, come to me, and by coming, undo the wrong you did me on earth.' I am sitting in the cemetery now on one of the low, altar-like tombs, writing, with a pocket inkstand laid out upon my solemn seat. I feel I shall not make many entries more. The volume is nearly concluded; so is my Book of Life hastening to its solemn Finis.

"Still that gentle voice comes more and more palpably, more and more forgivingly to my ear. There is no horror in it now; and, as it comes, it recalls to my mind a passage in Manning's exquisite sermon on 'The Sleep of the Faithful Departed.' Picturing the ecstatic reunion in the next world of those who had been separated here, he imagined the newly arrived one on the farther shore saying 'What, were you so often near us, and yet we did not see you?

There were times when we thought you were with us; but we looked around, and saw nothing. We listened, and all was still.' I quote from memory, but that is the substance of the sentences. I listened—oh, so intently, but, when I listened, I heard nothing. Directly I cease to listen consciously and begin to write again, I hear that loving voice calling me once more by the old familiar name. It was by the simple mention of a name, I remember, Magdalene recognised the Loved and Lost One.

"I can fancy Mr. Alexander Lund laughing consumedly at the change that has come over this narrative. That is part of my purgation, no doubt; just as aspiring writers have to pay for the honour of authorship by being criticised by some very small literary hack in a review. Let them rave!

"My landlady has become so very marked in her attentions that she walks out in the cemetery and brings her friends to admire

my devotion. I notice that several of them
are widows and many of them marriageable
maidens. Perhaps they think my grief is
capable of alleviation by them. I must
move. I am always striking my tent now,
like the Bedouin in the desert. I shall
soon strike it for the last time.

"I begin to debate the pros and cons of
suicide, and can pretty well forecast the
issue. My only dread is lest self-murder
should separate me from her in the next
world. When I am thinking seriously on
the subject, the voice, which I always hear
now, seems to take a sadder tone, almost
one of deprecation. It never says 'No, no;'
it only keeps repeating my name. All day
long, all the long sleepless nights it is the
same, 'Percy, Percy!' But when I reply
'I am coming to you, Mary,' the voice no
longer seems to call, but to warn.

"With fear and trembling I took an
afternoon train and came as near as I could
to Zoar, walking the rest of the distance
during the night. I came by *the spot* in

the very early morning, and really do not know why I did not end matters then. Simply, I believe, because I wanted to finish this volume, and write a direction which would enable some one to find it. I am quite resolved now that I will leave life as she left it, and where she left it. I will die the very death she did, and in the same place. If I drown myself with this volume upon me, it may be long before my body is found, and the record would have perished. I will simply keep upon my person a scrap, of paper directing them where to find this in words which will be enigmatical to all but Lund. I will assume that he finds this volume and is the first to read it. I will add nothing maudlin, but simply say I have forgotten my old grudge to him, and ask him, as soon as he can, to forgive me."

" Well, that's satisfactory so far, isn't it?" said Briggs.

"Very. How nervous this kind of reading makes one. I could have sworn *I* saw a human shadow, then."

" It's the ghost, no doubt.　Finish."

" There is very little more."

" The last night I spent on earth I spent in that nest where I found out you and Elsie used to meet when you know you had no right to meet her, Lund.　But I know now that these matters are not at our own disposal.　They are arranged for us, and we vainly fight against them.　So I do not upbraid you for taking my destined wife from me.　It is better as it is.

" There again, in the dead deep night, sleeping under God's open sky, I heard the voice, and there seemed to be no deprecation in it then.　I not only heard, but saw. Yes, out there in the darkness—the grey morning is only beginning to break as I write this—I saw that girlish face, girlish now no more, but radiant with heavenly beauty.　I know now that the so-called dead do live, and that we rejoin them directly we cast aside these fleshy tenements.　It is my only anxiety now, to be ' out of the body.'　Very likely my act may

be a wrong and wicked one. Possibly—
nay probably—I ought to wait for man's
justice to do slowly what—with my wonted
impetuosity—I proceed to do at one sharp
decisive stroke. It is for others rather
than for myself I do it; though I myself
am, I own, anxious to make the passage
quickly and quietly. The dawn is beginning to streak the horizon yonder, and
my purpose will be frustrated if I wait. I
see the grand old cathedral lying among
the mists in the valley—see my father's
grand house at Topaz, about which all this
fuss has been made, and which, no doubt, I
shall haunt like an unquiet shade. I must
add no more. I go on my last walk amid
these glorious woods—go to join Mary.
She is calling me still. I come, I come."

"And so ends the strange, eventful
history, does it?" asked Briggs, his voice
breaking in as incongruously upon the
romantic details as the applause of the
people succeeds some mystic melody in an
opera.

" Yes, that's all. What shall we do with the volume ?"

" Hand it over to the police, of course."

" Of course."

" Why Briggs, you are very eccentric this morning. The narrative has put you in a ghostly frame of mind. Why do you say 'of course' twice, and the second time so very much like that spectral gentleman in Hamlet ?"

" Pardon me, Lund, but I was just thinking the same of you, and was going to ask you why *you* repeat my words 'of course' in so very ghostly a tone."

" Then it *is* a ghost. Very well, we'll settle it so. Now the question I want to propound to you, Briggs, and to his ghost-ship if he be present, is : What am I to do with this MS. ?"

No reply this time from ghost or man.

" If I make it public by giving it up to the police, the chances are a hundred to one that there will be a verdict of *felo de se* at the coroner's inquest. You could not call that the work of a man even temporarily insane."

" Coroners' juries are very elastic in their verdicts," suggested Mr. Briggs.

" So they are; but to what purpose would be the exposé? Either I will pocket the volume, and say nothing about it, or—which I think would be better — let's cremate it on the spot."

" Burn it?"

" Burn it, if you like that better."

Then the mysterious shadow was explained in the most unromantic manner.

" No, that I'm hanged if you do," said the police-sergeant, clambering rapidly down the limestone rocks. " I haven't dodged you all this way, and listened patiently to that long story, which I thought never would end, to have it burnt before my eyes. I can claim it if I like, you know."

" Upon my word, sergeant, I compliment you on your skill and activity," said Lund. " I had no idea the London police could rise to the occasion so satisfactorily. Of course you can claim it, but cui bono ?"

" What's that ?"

" Who, as I asked, will be any the better for the exposé ?"

" Nobody. If you will give me your word you won't burn it, I will have been blind and deaf for the last two hours."

" That I will do freely."

" You never know—as Sam says—when a thing may come in useful."

" Your family novel, to wit," suggested Briggs.

" Ah, I had forgotten that."

" And don't you ever rail at the English police again in your articles. If you do, I shall be tempted to mention how you tried to mislead me by pretending not to understand the few words in that dead man's pocket; but I knew you did understand them, and kept my eye on you until I discovered what they were all about. Get your French police to beat that if they can."

"I am sure Fouché himself never did a better stroke of business."

"I don't know who that gentleman is, but I know many worse mornings' works have got a man a move at Scotland Yard."

"I shall have to write this matter up, you know, sergeant, for the London press. Depend upon it I will not forget to mention the almost preternatural sagacity with which our well-known sergeant —— of Bow Street pounced down upon the place where the murderer made away with himself."

"Very well; only qualify that term murderer with some such word as probable, or assumed, because, you know, in the absence of that volume, we have no right to know he *was* the murderer."

So the three went back to Zoar, as from a simple constitutional walk; and the two friends, giving it out that they had been lionizing the London sergeant in the rustic environs of the little city, suppressed all mention of the Murderer's Journal.

CHAPTER IV.

THE LAST NEW THING IN RELIGIONS.

NINE days' wonders soon blow over, even in a little place like Zoar, and when the coroner's jury had found that Percy Llewellyn destroyed himself while suffering from temporary insanity, and he had been duly interred in the family vault at St. Hilda's, Zoar society soon settled back into its state of stagnation once more. It was a curious index to the state of public opinion in Zoar, that nobody was at all surprised at the turn things had taken. They had always said it would happen so. They never thought there was any good in that parson, and so on. It is astonishing how many ex post facto prophets always start into active practice on such occasions. Nobody recollects their having indulged in the vaticinations they claim until after the event; but they say they did, and if they do not know, who should?

With the exception of Edward and Sam Llewellyn everybody was satisfied at the solution of the difficulty; perhaps even these were better pleased than they chose to confess; but Edward wrung his fat hands and lamented to his deaf wife, who could not hear him, the rude disruption of their day-dreams; and Sam was chiefly vexed that Percy should have turned out a fool as well as a knave after all.

"I'm glad there was no hanging in the matter," said the money-lender, "because examples of that kind are apt to be contagious."

Had Sam anything in the place where his conscience ought to have been, which made him tremble for his own neck in case of the halter being quartered among the arms of the Llewellyn family? They do not hang for the slow murder of Sixty per Cent. Men may murder the widow and the fatherless with impunity as long as they do it with such legal "instruments" as a bill of sale, or an "execution;" but Sam spoke so feelingly that it really sounded as though he must have been employing certain less legitimate methods of shortening some of his many victims' existence.

"It shows how little one can know of people," he continued. "From the nature of my business I am not in the habit of looking merely on the surface, but I was misled in Percy, Edward, that I was. I didn't think he had a soft place in him."

"But you see he had. I suppose you have got one somewhere, Sam."

"Edward! what do you mean?" He spoke with a tone of injured innocence, such as a man might assume if he were suddenly accused of having horns and a tail, or any other diabolical appendages.

"You must have had when you made up to Patty at all events."

"You know better. You know it was a stroke of policy on my part. I thought

Evangelical opinions would pay better than living hand and glove with the young fellows as I had been doing. Besides, it was expensive. Collections in church and subscription-lists run high too, but they're nothing compared with what it costs to go the pace with the young fellows you bleed."

"Percy's Evangelicalism was no more a sign of softness than yours."

"No; I didn't mean to insinuate that it was. De mortuis nil nisi bonum; but I'm very much afraid he lost his heart to that milliner, and so did what was perhaps the best thing he could under the circumstances, pitched himself neck and crop into the water after her."

"Yes, I suppose things are best as they are. If it hadn't been for that fellow Lund, Elsie and Percy would have been married, and all would have been square by this time perhaps."

"It's a maxim with me, when I *am* dead beat—it ain't very often—but when I am, to confess it, realise the fact, and act upon it."

"It's wise, perhaps."

"No perhaps at all about it. Yes, Lund licked you in re Elsie, and also in the matter of Phillis's will. That was a flea-bite, truly, but still we were licked. You see I identify myself with your interests, my dear brother, and say 'we,' not 'you.'"

"Yes, but don't 'dear brother' me in private. It sounds as though I were a client, and you thought you were taking me in."

"It's for the sake of practice. If I didn't snivel in private sometimes, I could never keep up my tone in public. That's where Patty is so useful."

"As your fellow-sniveller?"

"Yes. Now accepting your defeat in minor matters for a fact, you have, of course, under your arrangements, to beat this fellow Lund in bigger things."

"Of course."

"There's a half-hearted way about your saying that which makes me doubt you,

Edward ; and mind, I've a right to a word in this matter, because——"

" Because you've advanced money—at the usual rate—I know. Well what guarantee do you want ?"

" Simply that you will fight Topaz to the last gasp."

" Do you think I'm likely to cry 'peccavi,' and retire to the almshouse ?"

" There was a whining tone about your last remark but one or two which really would have justified me in harbouring such an idea."

" Why shouldn't I practise voluntary humility in private, as well as you snivel in secret ?"

" Oh, I see. Ah, that's good," exclaimed Sam, rubbing his hands. He was such an inbred hypocrite that he was overjoyed to find others following in his steps.

" The first shot has been fired in what is likely to be a hot campaign," said Edward, tossing him a legal document.

" A notice of ejectment served by Shep-

pard at the instance of William Llewellyn !
Yes, that looks like business. I like that.
It was, of course, inevitable. Now we are
in the right groove."

"It may go against us."

"It will, if you begin to think so. I
thought you had arranged the dates on
those wills, and that the acceptances we
hold of William's would cover all possible
expenses."

"True; but still you and I know that
the law is a lottery, and it may—I simply
say it *may*—go against us."

"Not if hard swearing will do anything."

"Perjury is risky sometimes."

"Not when artistically done. Your
bunglers and bad characters run risks, not
your professor of the art, not the possessor
of such a character as mine."

So the matter dropped for the time being.

Alec Lund, flattering himself that he had
been preternaturally active in firing this
first shot, fell back into the old groove in

London too. Sheppard was not in a hurry; and, to say the truth, Elsie and her husband dreaded the uncongenial atmosphere of a law-court. Without conceding their rights, they were content to be leisurely in asserting them; indeed, in his final interview with the Dean before leaving Zoar, Lund had noticed a certain air of mystery imported into the matter by the little dignitary, who thus dismissed him to his wife and duties.

" Return, Mr. Lund, and make our most kind compliments to your wife. Be content to wait for a very little while—as you have waited with exemplary patience already. I have one or two matters to consult Sheppard about, and think I see my way to arranging yours satisfactorily. By the way, would you mind leaving me that curious MS. volume you and Briggs spoke of? I know you are naturally anxious to show it to your wife; and, believe me, I appreciate your delicate anxiety that it should not be made public. It shall not without your express permission. But I see you are still unwilling to part with it. Retain it. Briggs, you say, knows its contents. Promise me only that when I summon you to Zoar, you will take the trouble to run down and bring it with you."

"Take it, by all means, my dear sir. I only feel a sort of responsibility about the volume. It was so evidently, though not, I own, avowedly, committed to my keeping by the dead man."

"You are quite right; and, on second thoughts, I wish you to retain it. Go now, or you will lose your train, and don't forget to think over those two or three controversial matters I mentioned."

"Forget!"

So Alec Lund went back to town, to his wife and heir and quill-driving once more; and one of the first articles he wrote was in laudation of the great intelligence displayed by the police in clearing up the mystery of the Zoar murder.

The only person not disposed to rest and

be thankful with the existing condition of things was Mr. Thomas Moddle. Neither sacred nor secular matters throve with him. He had failed signally in his matrimonial schemes. Not only so, but he had been dreadfully laughed at. Mrs. Fane herself, who would not hear of his being angry, asked him to dinner, and, as he could not help feeling, treated him with quiet contempt. She would even allude in public —that is, before the assembled circle of our dramatis personæ—to his hymeneal plans.

"I confess, Mr. Moddle, I behaved shamefully. Mea culpa — mea maxima culpa. But then, you see, Percy had to be found out, and all is fair, not only in love and war, but in police strategy; don't you think so?"

"Perhaps," said poor Moddle, looking sheepish.

"And then I did you the greatest kindness one person could do another, did I not?"

"How?"

"I saved your poor soul from perdition, by making a convert of you."

But Thomas Moddle could not and did not see this. He was as much disappointed in his ambition as in his love. In fact love and ambition blended very curiously in his consciousness, or the line of demarcation between them was faint and shadowy. With the Irvingites he had been a power— a triton among the minnows—almost an angel, in the ordinary as well as the technical acceptation of the word. At Zoar he had the reputation of being a scholar, and was the cynosure of admiring deaconesses and devoted members of his little flock. It was even known that he stood well with the regular clergy of the Established Church, and could have been admitted to Anglican Orders whenever he chose to give up the revived apostolate, and recognise in the Right Reverend the Lord Bishop of Zoar, throned in palatial state, the living embodiment and representative of the Scripless Twelve.

When he "went over," he thought he should have leapt at once into a position of eminence and profit. The Cardinalate would not have appeared to him beyond his deserts had he been in Roman Orders. He would blushingly but unhesitatingly have accepted the Popedom if offered to him. No overtures, however, were made in this direction; and he even went so low as to envy William Llewellyn's unremunerative and exacting office. His blood boiled when he saw his friend in a correct cassock, arranging the flowers on the altar and in the sanctuary for a great festival; whereas, when he even volunteered as beadle or pew-opener he was snubbed, and Father Blank thought it would be better to leave the duties to be performed by the officials. Evidently no great faith was put in Moddle's conversion; not even so much as in Alec Lund's. Mrs. Fane, of course, was in the odour of sanctity, and even William Llewellyn was looked on as promising : but Moddle was eyed askance,

and Moddle's soul resented the treat-
ment.

He would have liked to come back—to
be a *re-'vert*—but dared not.   Besides, had
he done so, it is more than doubtful whether
he would have found his old place open to
him ; for the Catholic Apostolic Church was
no friend to Rome, though she had—perhaps because she had—so closely assimilated
her system to a Roman model   It is, in
fact, a kind of fusion between Judaism and
Romanism.   So Mr. Moddle set his wits to
work to strike out a new and original line
for himself.   He was a disciple in search of
a religion.   He ran through the whole
graduated scale of the recognised faiths, but
found some objection in each.

The Greek Church he would have liked,
principally on account of its assumed title
of " orthodox ;" for, with all his cleverness,
Mr. Moddle was one with whom words
went for a good deal—sometimes so much
as to stand in place of the things they represented.   But the Holy Eastern Church

was a goal beyond hope. He was sorry to think so, because fraternization in this direction was fashionable, and if he could only have seen his way to becoming an archimandrite, he would have sacrificed a good deal. He more than ever regretted his precipitation in leaving the Catholic Apostolic Church, because the name of "Angel" went so very far. Many people believed him an angel in nature as well as in name. However, each of these bodies was quite out of range.

Anglicanism—well, that might do as a last resource. He preferred something out of the beaten track. He was one of those eccentric beings who suit a persecuted rather than a triumphant faith. The persecution must be very mild, for Moddle had no notions of martyrdom; but he was democratic in his tastes, and did not like to feel other men much bigger than himself.

Wesleyanism and Congregationalism in its different forms he thought of, but put aside. He had a notion that they were vulgar, and he had begun, since he aspired to Mrs. Fane, to affect ton in his religion. He would none of these. Positivism, with the Comtist ritual revived, occupied his attention very seriously. A ninefold sacramental system, and a complicated cultus which nobody understood very much about, was the line upon which his thoughts ran.

So he fell to reading the Positivist Catechism ; yet still found details which did not please him. His system must be eclectic, but—as far as compilation made it so—his own. It should be in nature, though not by name, Moddle-ism.

First of all he secured the services of Mr. William Llewellyn, about whom he had all along been hovering, even before his ideas took any definite shape ; and he soon succeeded in alienating that easy-going personage from his duties as sacristan.

" It's all very well to call you a sacristan, William," said Mr. Moddle, in a tone of playful irony, " but they seem to give you the work of a beadle and a bell-ringer combined. If they only threw in a little grave-digging, they might as well call you sexton as sacristan."

"I'm satisfied."

"No, you're not." Mr. Moddle had a habit of contradicting people flatly when he wanted to carry a point. "Do you mean to tell me the menial duties which come upon you are as much befitting your powers as when you were an Evangelist in the Catholic Apostolic Church? Think of those charming ten-minutes sermonettes you used to give us in Zoar; whereas all your time is wasted now in sticking flowers in vases or arranging dips on the altar."

"Ha!"

"Of course I know you don't like it. You can't. You say it's better to be a door-keeper, &c., and as an exercise of humility that's all very well; but the human must be separated from the divine element in the Church, and it's the human, not the divine element that has made you a sacristan, and keeps me a layman."

"What do you propose to substitute?"

"I have received an illumination."

"A what?" asked Mr. Llewellyn, his thoughts running on altar candles, probably.

"An inspiration. All ideas are inspirations; but this has been so forced in upon me that I feel it would be wrong to suppress it."

"Don't by any means; at all events until you have communicated with me. What is it?"

Then did Mr. Moddle unfold to that attentive neophyte his grand idea of an eclectic religion, which should borrow from all sources from the Catholics to the Ranters.

"There is," he said, "good in all, bad in all; and the duty of the individual is to choose the good, and refuse the evil."

"You forget we have merged the right to do that when we joined the Church, and ignored private judgment."

"No, I don't forget it; but *can* we ignore private judgment? Did you or I ignore private judgment when we joined the Church ?"

"Since you ask the question, I rather think we both of us did."

"How so?"

"I was greatly led by Alec, my son-in-law."

"And I?"

"By Mrs. Fane.   Was it not so?"

"Perhaps it was."   Strange as it seemed, since he had not by any means come off with flying colours in his love-affair, Mr. Moddle rather liked being joked about it; certainly liked talking it over in private. Did he still entertain hopes in the direction of the fascinating widow?   Perhaps.   His heart was a very elastic one, indeed, almost as elastic as his conscience.

Here was a chance, at all events, for Moddle to make himself the head of a sect, dress up in purple and fine linen, and possibly fare sumptuously every day.   There was no chance of this under a Catholic régime.   He was nowhere; and he did not like being nowhere. He had an extreme aversion to being left out in the cold, and lately his existence had been arctic.

"If we could only raise a little money and rent a chapel—buying a lease is out of the question, for I am at the end of my tether—I'll guarantee we two together could make the thing go splendidly. You should have a far finer altar than you have at present, grander flowers, and more dips. What do you think of that?"

"An altar without a sacrifice!"

"Precisely. I believe that would take. Hundreds of people like the æsthetics of Catholicism or Ritualism who hate their essence. Why not give them the shadow without the substance?"

"Does it not seem like playing at Church?"

"Perhaps. But then come to statistics. What do the great majority of people go to Church for? Is it anything more than play?"

"It's respectable."

"And we will be eminently respectable. Why, man," continued the ex-angel, warming with his subject, "the Liberation Society ought to take the best chapel in London for me, and pay handsomely for the idea as well. Nothing would bring down the old Establishment so soon as the setting up these private chapels all over the country."

"But would they do any good?"

"Honestly I believe they would. They would wage a sort of guerilla warfare against irreligion. Privateering has gone out of fashion; but there have been times when privateers have done as good service as the regular fleet."

"And plundered on their own account too."

"And plundered on their own account too, if you like to call it plunder. But why it should be called plunder on the part of an individual, and fair prize-money when it is extorted by an organized band, I cannot quite comprehend."

"Humph!"

"The doctor and lawyer once qualified can set up for themselves. Why not the parson?"

"Only we ain't qualified."

"Then start as quacks. I don't care what they call me."

"As long as it pays?"

"As long as my conscience tells me I am doing good, and I get a fair week's wage for an honest week's work. What say you to the scheme?"

"I'll think about it."

Mr. William Llewellyn did think about it, and thought favourably. Mr. Moddle felt sure of him when he said so much. Mr. Llewellyn had never had the courage to say "No," decidedly in his life, certainly not to Mr. Moddle, and scarcely to anybody else. Perhaps he would have thriven better if he had.

So Mr. Moddle put an advertisement in the *Echo* and got a small chapel, down a slummy street at a weekly rent which in-

volved no serious risk and necessitated little
outlay. By means of a speculative printer,
he had himself placarded all over the
neighbourhood as the "minister"—that
seemed a good via media title between
priest and pastor—while animated sand-
wiches paraded the streets with large
posters, and distributed handbills, containing the titles of an inflammatory series
of sermons to be preached in the "School of
Tyrannus," as he called it, by the Rev.
Thomas Moddle, Ex-Angel of the Catholic
Apostolic Church. In these discourses he
proposed to discuss the weak points of all
the existing sects seriatim, and invite their
members to "come out" in favour of
Eclectic Christianity. The evening sermon
was to be followed by discussion, and all the
services were to be choral and ornate to the
last degree.

"Rowland Hill wanted to know why the
devil was to have all the pretty tunes. I
want to know why the Pope should
monopolise all the nice flowers, incense

and candles. He shall not, if I know it."

"I think I can trim your chancel for you," said William Llewellyn; "but it's as ugly as sin to begin with."

"All the more room for your art. By the way isn't that name for the chapel a triumph—the School of Tyrannus? I was divided between that and "The House of Justus," which you will recollect "joined hard by the synagogue;" but I thought people at large mayn't remember that circumstance, and it would make it too long if I put those words in the title. Otherwise they might think Justus was some mediæval saint."

But there was another feature in Mr. Moddle's scheme which was still more unique, and on which he calculated to make his new religion "draw." The whole thing was to be done by women, with the exception of himself and William Llewellyn. The choir in the western gallery was composed of females possessing good voices, who came for a very modest sum weekly. Men, he found, were dearer; so he discovered that women were much more devotional. He also found out, however, that the women who could sing were generally plainer than those who could not. As a rule the real vocalists would not bear inspection; so he had a dozen of the pretty ones grouped in the apsed chancel around himself, while he sat vested in the most nondescript attire, a regular Jack-among-the-maidens, and relegated the ugly ones with voices to the western gallery, where they were stowed away behind a curtain, to be heard but not seen.

There was a small dwelling-house attached to this School of one Tyrannus where Mr. Moddle took up his abode; and it was astonishing what an amount of work it required in the way of rehearsals before the thing could be got to go smoothly. When this was accomplished it certainly made good the proverb that whatever new sect may be started is sure to find some adherents. The School became a positive Cave of Adullam for the dissatisfied and the ineligible of all the different sects and communities of Christendom as represented in the great metropolis; and very vigorous indeed were the debates which ensued upon the Sunday evening sermons, so much so that Mr. Moddle was fain to register his little conventicle and prevent a breach of the peace by having an awakened policeman at hand in case of emergency. The thing certainly promised well at first.

"William, I mean to make this go," was the remark of the ex-angel as he counted out a very satisfactory collection in the little vestry after service.

"Yes," replied Mr. Llewellyn, timidly, "it seems to take, but——"

"Then why in the world insert that most objectionable conjunction? If it answers, what would you have more?"

"How about Father Blank and the authorities in general?"

"I don't care a straw for them.   Do you?"

"Well, yes, I rather do, you know."

"Then by all means go back to them. No—I really don't mean this as a taunt. If you are only half-hearted, and if you feel this sort of thing will not suit either your conscience or your pocket, give it up.   I would much rather work singlehanded than with one who is not in earnest.   It is most depressing."

Mr. Llewellyn remained silent; and Moddle proceeded to try a little dexterous flattery.

"Your loss in one sense would be irreparable—I don't mind confessing that to so old a friend as you are.   That grouping of the twelve young ladies who can't sing, with their white dresses and long flowing hair around the floral altar with lights, drapery, and incense, was simply perfect."

"I'm glad you liked it," said Mr. Llewellyn, softening.

"Liked it!   why it was a study for an

artist, and it filled the whole of the reserved seats of itself, quite irrespective of the service, sermon, or discussion."

And yet, despite this free confession, Mr. Moddle allowed his colleague to work simply as an amateur; and Mr. William Llewellyn was very much too simple-minded to think of asserting his rights boldly. So he fell back on his fear of the authorities, which was quite true, only it was not all the truth.

"I know what it is, William," continued Moddle; "Lund has been tampering with you."

"I don't think I should use the word tampering, if I were you, because it's offensive. True, both Lund and Father Blank have spoken to me seriously, as good Catholics are bound to do."

"And Mrs Fane?"

"She thinks the scheme might be utilised for purposes of proselytism—as a sort of decoy to Rome."

"Not a bad idea."

“ In which case she would only be too
glad to join your unseen chorus, and to
allow Amy to add to the charms of the
visible choir; but it must be permissu
superiorum.”

“ Which permission she would never get.
No, I hate the dilatory tricks and sloth of
Rome.   I have had enough of it.”

“ Yes, you didn’t seem to run well in
harness.”

“ Harness!   They never gave me a
chance : but I’ll thin their numbers for
them.”

“ I thought you were not going to be
aggressive,” remarked Mr. Llewellyn, who
was the veriest peace-at-any-price man.

“ Opposition to Rome always pays,” was
the shrewd reply of Mr. Moddle.

This pecuniary character of the scheme
was extremely grating to Mr. Llewellyn,
though he himself gained nothing by the
new scheme.   Moddle’s one thought, or, at
all events, his first thought, was always—
Will such a thing draw ?   Will it pay ?

When reasoned with he would point to other religious bodies, notoriously, as he averred, to Rome and the Established Church. "Look at these," he would say. "Is not their one end and aim to make money? The Establishment, true to its name, is simply a great trading firm, which tries to keep a monopoly of the loaves and fishes by means of its parochial system. Why have the lawyers and the doctors no parochial systems, I should like to know?"

"But we have nothing to do with the Establishment," Mr. Llewellyn would mildly suggest. "We have come out from that, at all events."

"But is your Cardinal one whit less worldly than the Primate of All England? True, he does get himself up ecclesiastically in a scarlet train, instead of jack-boots and yellow driving-gloves, and has some show of apostolical succession to back up his pretensions; but put either of them—Cardinal-Archbishop, or Archibald of Canterbury—alongside one of those from whom they claim succession, and is there one trait, one lineament of likeness? Wouldn't either the one or the other cut Peter, primus apostolorum, dead in the street to-morrow, if he dared, in his fisherman's garb, approach the luxurious carriage of my Lord Archbishop, or his Eminence the Cardinal? Psha! I don't go in for humility or disinterestedness myself, but I am not such a blatant undisguised hypocrite as either of these."

This seemed to do Mr. Moddle good; and he often let off the steam thus, both in private and in public. It acted as a sort of safety-valve.

" What I want to get, is one good, substantial, addle-headed old woman, such as Fate seems to send so abundantly to Spurgeon. Look at him again. Where is the difference between Tait at Lambeth, or Manning at Westminster, and this popeling of Newington Tabernacle and Nightingale Lane? Why, this fellow, on the strength of his bluff exterior, and his consummate mastery of the English language (which I grant) is domesticated like a prince. His aviary is larger than any sitting-room you or I ever had. And yet this is pure gospel religion. I tell you once more, sir, the thing don't exist. It went out with the apostolic age; and miracles, of course, ceased with it."

"Why not revive that?"

"So I did—or tried to; and found there was just as big a scramble to get among the apostolic band in Gordon Square, as ever there was to secure an Anglican Bishopric or a seat in the College of Cardinals. It's money from beginning to end, though the things are not advertised as so much property, like Church livings in the *Ecclesiastical Gazette;* but we should come to that—I mean the Irvingites would—in a very few years, if they were the dominant sect. Fancy buying the position of angel, or being made an apostle for a consideration!"

"But the miracles at least were genuine."

" Yes, they were. It's as well you put it in the past tense. It was all a matter of enthusiasm. As long as Irving's personal influence lasted, prophecy flourished, and 'tongues' were frequent. When that influence waned, it all went out like a damp squib on a wet fifth of November."

" And will not the same fate attend the School of one Tyrannus, think you?"

" I don't think; I'm sure of it. Hence my resolve to make hay while the sun shines. As soon as my influence wanes," said this modest ex-angel, " so soon will the benches of the Tyrannus School be empty. The pretty girls won't draw. Even your artistic altar will cease to be effective. It is the enthusiasm that keeps the thing going. From the Pro-Cathedral down to Moody and Sankey, it is all one—a huge money speculation, kept going by the energy of the directors. This is a low view to take of a so-called religious system, you may say; but it is a wonderfully true one, and you know it in your inner consciousness, don't you?"

It was wonderful to see what a spell the one man did exercise over the other, much as that other differed in sentiment and opinion from him in detail. It was an instance in support of Moddle's own assertion, how much might be done even by a nature that had no actual right of superiority, given only self-reliance and energy—it was scarcely worthy the name of enthusiasm.

Certainly the School of Tyrannus flourished bravely for some time. The services were bright and musical, each an olla podrida of the most marvellously different materials. You were always coming across something you least expected, from the time when Moddle entered to soft music, habited in short surplice, coloured cassock and stole, girt with his attendant damsels in white, down to the time when he mounted the pulpit in Geneva gown and bands, and after long extempore prayer, delivered a sermon where St. John Chrysostom divided the honours with John Calvin and Robertson and Maurice were intimately blended with Keble and John Henry Newman. As a piece of eclecticism it was perfect. The only danger Moddle seemed to run was, lest in trying to please everybody he should please nobody, and so displease himself most of all.

On a Sunday evening the sermon would be a polemical one. It was, in fact, a short paper—for Moddle read it, and then circulated it in the chapel for the modest sum of one penny—devoted to showing up the weak points of some one system or absence of system. Of course all the disciples of that particular school mustered in force armed to the teeth for the purpose of defending their own particular ism and proving that their one doxy exhausted orthodoxy.

"Not so, my good friends," Moddle would say, and he said it with slight variety of diction every Sunday until it became quite as much a matter of course as the " Dearly beloved brethren" at which he was fain to poke his fun. " Yours is a very good doxy; really, as times go, a very respectable doxy indeed; but you have not ultimated truth. Your doxy wants another doxy to make it symmetrical. Happiness was born a twin, and Adam found even Paradise dull until he mated his doxy with Eve's doxy. That is exactly what we seek to do here—to fuse and blend all the different forms of Christian thought. I say Christian, my friends, not at all as excluding other forms of faith than Christianity. I simply feel that these are foreign to my field of thought. Buddhism, to wit, is a beautiful system, and its points of contact with Christianity are numerous and also exceedingly curious; but it would open up far too wide a subject if we wandered beyond the pale of Christianity. We are born Christians, let us adorn our profession."

So saying, or saying something to this effect, he would glide down the pulpit stair, and while a hymn was being sung, and the inevitable collection made (though the reserved seats were let at a high tariff, and the others were nowhere), he would divest himself of his preacher's gown, and taking a seat below the pulpit, constitute himself chairman of the debate which ensued. Combining thus in his own person the opposite characters of advocate and judge, it was no marvel that Moddle generally got the best of the argument. If he did not, and the disputants became noisy or questioned his right to occupy the chair while maintaining one set of opinions only, the lights were gently lowered, the awakened policeman came to the front, and the debate was declared to be either closed or adjourned.

Moddle made a good many enemies in this way; but he made friends too. He was one of those men who excited violent sympathies or antipathies. You never found a person who liked Moddle a little, or disliked him only a little. They idolized or abominated him; and he gloried in the knowledge that this was the case. "Let me have light or darkness," he used to say, "I hate your neutral tints. Nothing is so effective as a good chiaroscuro." If the man's power had been tempered with a little more refinement, he had a good many of the elements which go to make up a successful heresiarch.

His heresy did succeed; but the success was transient, and the collapse came from a most unexpected quarter. He was vexed beyond measure that Alec Lund, and especially that his old pupil Elsie, treated his scheme with quiet indifference. If Lund would only have written him down in a stinging leader he would have been well content; but the ordeal of silence he could not complacently undergo.

William Llewellyn dangled as was his wont, helplessly between Catholicism and Eclecticism—such was the only appellation Moddle would allow to be applied to his system. He would willingly have broken with Moddle altogether, and he told Mrs. Fane so when she had been rating him soundly for the hundredth time on the score of his schismatic tendencies.

"I shall simply get Father Blank to ex-communicate you, if you don't either give Moddle up, or use him as a tool for getting converts to the Church."

"The Church made a great mistake in snubbing Moddle," was Mr. Llewellyn's re-joinder.

"Excuse me, the Church never makes mistakes. She is infallible, and couldn't make mistakes if she tried. I snubbed Mr. Moddle too, you know. I hate him."

"You don't."

"I do."

"You don't," replied William Llewellyn, more forcibly than was his wont.

"Mr. Llewellyn!"

"Mrs. Fane."

"Do you mean to tell me I don't know my own mind?"

"You couldn't put my opinion into better

English. That's exactly what I do mean to say."

"Then, to prove that you are wrong, I will tell you what I will do. I will crush this scheme of Moddle's."

"Moddle's! You see you call him by his ungarnished name. Call him Thomas—or Tommy—at once."

"Mr. Llewellyn, don't be irritating. I tell you I hate Mr. Moddle——"

"Tommy——"

"And I've only got to put my finger on this newfangled scheme of his to make it tumble down about his ears like a child's card house; and I'll do it too."

"Of course you will."

"Of course I will! What is the man sniggling at now? Amy, my dear, look and see whether you discern any lurking signs of insanity in this person. What were those visiting justices doing when they interfered with such admirable family arrangements, and let this exceedingly dangerous lunatic loose on society?"

"I think he's harmless, mamma," answered Amy; and William Llewellyn sniggled still.

" Will you, or will you not tell me what you mean by that significant ' of course,' idiot?"

" Of course you'll smash up the School of one Tyrannus, get Moddle back into the odour of sanctity, and then——"

" What?"

" Marry him. Do you think he doesn't know the meaning of ' no,' whether it comes from an old lady or a young one ?"

" Amy, will you protect your mother? First he tells me I am making up to Mr. Moddle——"

" Tommy——"

" Be quiet! And then he calls me an old woman. *Am* I an old woman, Amy?"

" No, mamma, you are——" And Amy joined Mr. William Llewellyn in a mutual sniggle now.

" What am I ?"

" A nice marriageable widow lady, and worthy to be Mrs. Thomas Moddle."

Mrs. Fane was as good as her word; whether Mr. Llewellyn's appraisement of her motive was the true one remains to be seen. She made no secret of her propagandism; at least she gave it out openly that the end of saving souls justified the use of any means for its accomplishment; and saving souls, according to Mrs. Fane's theology, was simply folding them by any means, convinced or unconvinced, within the external pale of the Roman Church.

The policy she adopted was characteristic. After a certain evening service, though the debate had nothing in it to attract persons of the Roman persuasion, Father Blank unexpectedly put in an appearance at the chapel. He did not, it is true, attend the service; but he hung about as though he belonged to the place, and directly the discussion commenced he shook hands effusively with Moddle, and supported him at every point during the subsequent proceedings. The disputants got angry, and twitted Moddle about being hand and glove with a

Romish priest. Moddle devoutly wished Father Blank at the bottom of the sea; but, on his own principle of a clear stage and no favour, he could not refuse the alliance Father Blank so pointedly offered.

Down the chapel were Mrs. Fane and Amy, with another Romish ecclesiastic; and when the people went out they found two men delivering handbills inviting their presence at some Roman Catholic festival or other during the week. The debate was adjourned, and the Nonconformists (they were the Sandemanians, or some equally obscure sect), had been getting decidedly the worst in the argument. On the following Sunday, when the discussion was resumed, as soon as Moddle took the chair, a disputant got up and asked to be allowed to put a question. This was granted, and he simply inquired—

" Are you, sir, or are you not, a Roman Catholic?"

Moddle took high ground, and entirely denied the right of his interrogator to put such a question to him. He did not press it, but simply said, with ironical courtesy—

"Thank you, I require no answer. Your silence, and the presence of a Roman ecclesiastic last Sunday, are quite enough. I see what the School of Tyrannus is—a decoy for Rome. My course is plain. I retire from this controversy, and expect most of those present will do the same."

They did. They left en masse, and the thing got into the papers. Next Sunday there was a small congregation ; the following Sunday none at all. Shortly after the choir struck for wages—first the unpresentable vocalists, and next the ornamental young ladies. A destructive is always quicker than a constructive process ; and the destruction of the Tyrannus School was very rapid indeed. The last thing heard of it was that the pulpit and ornamental altar were distrained upon for rent.

So ended the very latest thing in religions; and, as Moddle meditated upon his brief day-dream in the seclusion of his suburban lodging, he soliloquized complacently between the puffs of his pipe—

"Sic transit gloria mundi! It lasted longer than I expected. Fancy that fascinating little widow going out of her way to tumble down Tyrannus. I like her ten times better than ever for her 'cuteness; and I'll marry her yet, or my name's not Thomas Moddle."

Will he?

CHAPTER V.

THE building of Mr. Edward Llewellyn's princely mansion on the site of the once humble farmhouse named Topaz, progressed a good deal faster than Mr. Sheppard's legal process of ejection. For some inscrutable reason the law's delay was more perceptible than ever in this matter; and the result was, Alec Lund was growing dissatisfied with, almost suspicious of, his man of business; and the proprietor of Topaz, as far as possession went, took courage, and believed that no proceedings would be commenced; that the notice of ejectment was only a flash in the pan, and that very probably Lund had never seen the will at all, but only made a shrewd guess, which happened to be right.

Clearly Mr. Edward Llewellyn was in a condition of judicial blindness.

Mr. Sheppard, on the contrary, though he seemed to sleep, was preternaturally wide awake, and simply watched, like a hawk, the moment to make his pounce. Hand and glove with him were the Dean and Precentor, and the Dean's wife was now added to their councils.

"You had better reopen your communications with Mrs. Fane, my dear," said the Dean. "You recollect the lady who sent supplies while the William Lunds were in difficulties?"

"I recollect. The Papist woman who turned Alec's head?"

"Never mind that, my dear, we'll soon turn it back again. It's screwed on the right way, but has just got a temporary twist. It's what we are all liable too."

"Not Romewards, let us hope."

"It might be very much worse. Let us thank goodness it *is* no worse. I will engage to bend the crooked stick straight in a very little time."

"I wish you success; but I fancy you miscalculate your man. What am I to say to this Mrs. Fane?"

"I should just tell her, in the most mysterious manner possible, and desiring her not to say one word to Alec or Elsie, that the Topaz matter will very soon be settled now, and can only be settled in one way; therefore it's probable that Elsie's connexion with her pupil will have to cease."

"It has, to some extent, I believe, since the advent of the baby. But will not Elsie think me meddlesome?"

"She will inevitably insist on giving three months' notice, if you don't do it for her in advance."

"Well, I will write."

"And I will go and see this dreadful lawyer before communicating with Sheppard. I know it's irregular; but I do like dispensing with lawyers, if possible."

This dialogue was carried on during the commencement of an afternoon drive; and the Dean was deposited at Mr. Edward Llewellyn's door, leaving his wife to continue her airing alone.

Generally affable and accessible enough, Mr. Edward Llewellyn had, since his son's death, shut himself up and led, so it was reported, the life of a recluse. The only occasion upon which he went abroad was when he paid visits to Topaz Farm, and inspected the building operations there. The gossips said he was anxious to retire thither and hide his wounded pride, his broken hopes, from the eyes of the little world of Zoar. It had been his plan, and he made but a poor secret of it, to instal Percy there as incumbent of St. Simon Magus. He said no; that he would rather Percy went and played the squire in the country; but everybody knew that Topaz was the coveted scene of his son's squiredom, if his family could only get on visiting terms with the cathedral dignitaries at Zoar. That was

Edward Llewellyn's one soft place; and he veiled it very transparently. First, however, came the disappointment of Elsie's marriage with Lund, and then the more stinging blow of Percy's ignominious death. Yet still some spell seemed on him to draw him to Topaz. He himself, perhaps, would reinstate the fallen fortunes of his family. He had no one else for whom to scheme now but himself and his deaf wife. Fate had written them childless.

Sam paid flying visits every now and then to Zoar, to cheer Edward up, as he said. Zoar was a very gossiping place; and the chatterers again hazarded a conjecture that Edward was inclined to cave in about the Topaz ejectment business, of which, of course, they were all aware; and that it required the constant presence of his brother to keep him up to the mark. Sometimes Patty ran down too, and then the two ladies would sit at home while the brothers walked up to Topaz, and saw how things were progressing.

Tho last scaffold-pole had been taken down from the exterior of the house on the very day when the Dean called at Edward Llewellyn's residence in Zoar. The decorators of the interior had kept pace, and were ready to make their exit too; in fact, nothing remained but for Edward Llewellyn to remove such of his Lares and Penates as he purposed to carry with him, and then to migrate himself, and begin squiredom in good earnest on his own account. Edward and Sam were sipping a glass of dry sherry in the front parlour, for their walk had wearied them, when the sudden stoppage of the decanal carriage, and deposition of the Very Reverend himself at the door startled each of them from his serenity, and evoked from Edward a simple expression of surprise, natural enough under the circumstances; while Sam, as was his custom in private life, wondered what in the name of his Satanic Majesty that little fool could want, garnishing the title of folly with a participle expressive of utter condemnation.

"Can he have heard that Topaz is complete, and have called in consequence?" thought Edward. "Has the Millennium dawned? Is the good time so long coming come at last?"

He certainly had called; and the servant was trying to entice him into the drawing-room, but the little man had a strong will of his own.

"I think, my good girl, if I may hazard a conjecture, Mr. Edward Llewellyn is in his private room here. I will wait in the hall; and you may save both him and me time if you ask whether he will see me there."

He had seen Edward and Sam closeted there before he disembarked.

"Come in, Mr. Dean, by all means," said Edward, emerging from the side parlour, and killing as much time as he could, while Sam put away the decanter and glasses, and trying to make his maidservant think he was hailfellow-well-met with the Dean.

"Very much obliged to you. I have just

arrived at that time of life that every unnecessary pair of stairs becomes a serious consideration. Besides, I want to speak to you in private—not as far as this gentleman is concerned," he continued as he entered, " for I believe I have the honour of shaking hands with Mr. Samuel Llewellyn, have I not?"

Sam said, bluntly, " Yes," he had.

" Delighted I am sure, Mr. Samuel Llewellyn; it is many years since we met. What I have to say is certainly not of a nature that should prevent your being present."

"I should think not," was the almost surly reply.

"And your surmise is quite correct. I come as a peacemaker."

"From Alec Lund, I'll be sworn," said Sam, interrupting.

" Be quiet, Sam," said Edward, who did not want to witness the disruption of his daydreams at the very moment of their realization.

“No, Mr. Llewellyn, not from Mr. Lund, not even from Mrs. Lund, but purely on my own account, though in their interest, I grant you.”

“It comes to the same thing.”

“I fear,” said the Dean, facing right round, and addressing himself exclusively to Edward, “that my visit is an unseasonable one. I will bring it to an end, and call at some other time.”

“Oh pray, Mr. Dean——” poor Edward began, deprecatingly, and made a hideous grimace at his outspoken brother.

“Let him say what he likes, then,” answered Sam, in response to this silent appeal, “I’ll say nothing;” and taking up a book, he began to read.

“I come, as I said,” continued the Dean, “in the interests of peace. There have been trials and troubles enough already, God knows.”

Poor Edward sighed sympathetically, and Sam sneered at him over his book for so doing.

"Would it be well to add another scandal by letting this Topaz business go into Court?"

"I don't want to go into Court," replied Edward. "I'm molesting no one. Why does Lund molest me? He hasn't a leg to stand on."

"Is it possible you forget the existence of this will of Mrs. Dash?" asked the Dean, with the utmost simplicity. "Do you not know that this will and that of Mr. Morris Llewellyn contradict each other in almost every particular?"

Sam began to scuffle his feet under the table as much as to say he could not bear this kind of thing much longer.

"That will all have to be proved," said Edward, timidly enough.

"The wills were drawn here. You *know* the proof is easy," rejoined the Dean.

"Strange that so much time has been lost," suggested Edward, "if the proofs were so simple."

"There may have been reasons for that.

Now come, can't you make some arrangement ?"

Edward hesitated; and Sam, shutting his
book with a bang, said—

"I say, Edward, if you can stand this
jesuitry, I can't.   It's as plain as daylight
to me.   These people, egged on by that
blackguard Sheppard, who knows he can
never get his costs without dispossessing
you, actually send the Dean here to get you
to commit yourself.   I don't want to say
anything uncivil, but I know the world, and
you, as a lawyer, ought to know enough of it
to be aware that this kind of thing is utterly
irregular.   All I propose is that we talk of
any other subject in the world except this
one of the Topaz estate.   It's in the hands
of the legal representatives on each side;
and for the parties themselves, or any go-
betweens to discuss it is in bad form, to say
the least of it."

"Go upstairs, and sit with Patty and
Mary Ann," urged Edward, really anxious
to propitiate the little dignitary, and get

him to stay a decent time, if only for the edification of the maidservant.

"Not at all, Mr. Llewellyn, don't let me separate you. On second thoughts, if you will allow me, since I hear the ladies are in the drawing-room, I *will* go up for a moment. Let me hope you will both accompany me; and, my dear Mr. Samuel, let us forget—as far as I am concerned—that this matter has been entered upon."

Up the little man went with the two brothers, and made himself so agreeable with them and their wives that when Patty had thoroughly got over his M.B. waistcoat and rigidly erect coat-collar they passed quite a pleasant half-hour, and all were sorry when they were informed that the carriage had called for their very reverend visitor.

Mrs. Dean only sent up cards.

"How fortunate I was here, Edward," said Sam, when the excitement was over. "That little humbug would have bamboozled you——"

"Into giving up Topaz? Do you really think so? Am I so very verdant?"

"Greenish," was the reply.

"But not so green as that; no, no. You have neglected, Sam, to cultivate the suaviter in modo, relinquishing it entirely in favour of the fortiter in re."

"Money-lending makes one very plain-spoken."

"And yet I've heard you soft enough where there was a job on hand."

"But there's nothing to be got out of this fellow by soft soap, as far as I can see."

"Yes, there is."

"What?"

"Mary Ann wants to visit at the Deanery."

"And look at Mary Ann's chance. The Dean's wife sends up pasteboards. Mary Ann will call at the Deanery. Mrs. Dean will be out—I'll bet ten to one she is. Mary Ann will drop *her* pasteboards, and there the matter will end; and for the sake of that you would temporize in the matter of Topaz."

"Temporize, yes; yield one inch, no."

"Can I trust you?"

"Am I sane?"

"No, but—honour bright—I've a stake in this matter as well as you. Do you promise me you'll concede nothing?"

"Of course I promise it. What folly to ask!"

"Very well, then, I'm satisfied," said Sam; but his looks belied him if he was.

It was necessary for Mr. Samuel Llewellyn to go back to town, as there were certain mortgages where he wanted to foreclose, sundry bills of sale, where the expressive rule of action for his myrmidons was to be "sell up." Numerous were the widows' houses thus to be devoured, for Sam's business was quite a speciality in being mixed up with minors and un-protected females. They gave far less trouble than grown-up men. They were

ready to sign anything; they would put
their names to any number of blank pieces
of paper, leaving them to be filled in by
Mr. Llewellyn; and sixty per cent. was the
very minimum rate he ever got from them.
But all this demanded personal care and
attention; so back he went to town, relying
on Edward's promise not to "square it" in
any way, but at the same time leaving
Patty behind with orders to telegraph
instantly if there were the slightest signs of
renewed overtures from the enemy.

But the little Dean was just as clever as
Sam himself, and read the money-lender's
tactics quite easily; so he did nothing at
all until Sam was quite clear of the place,
and then he did not call or send any
messenger who could be identified. He
would not even write himself, but got
Briggs to pen a few lines to Edward
Llewellyn which he sent through the post
marked "private" and simply requested him
to call at his earliest convenience at the
Deanery, as he wished to speak to him on a

matter connected with his late son, the Rev. Percy Llewellyn.

Edward quite fell into the snare. He thought that, as the living of St. Simon Magus had now lapsed by Percy's death, and the Dean had bought the presentation, he wanted to consult him on some details connected with the accounts, perhaps even to ask his advice in appointing Briggs to the incumbency. He was the more disposed to take this view from the circumstance of Briggs writing the letter; and when, on arriving at the Deanery, he found the writer there, he had no doubt at all that the precentor was to form the main subject of their conversation.

After the usual commonplaces had been exchanged the Dean boldly led up to the matter in hand.

" Mr. Llewellyn," he said, " do not think me unfeeling if I ask you whether you have any papers belonging to your late son—I am obliged to mention his name."

" You mean, of course, papers relating to

the church. In my capacity of church-
warden as well as patron the papers
naturally passed through my hands, and I
think, Mr. Dean, you will find everything
in perfect order——"

" As becomes one so intimately versed in
ecclesiastical matters ; I have not the
slightest doubt such will be the case. But,
pardon me, it was not entirely of that I was
thinking, though I shall be glad to recur to
it."

" Of what were you thinking, then ?"

" Have you any papers referring to the—
the death—either his own death, or that of
the poor girl ?"

" Mr. Dean, Mr. Dean !" exclaimed
Edward Llewellyn, in a tone of deprecation,
and holding his poor head just as William
did. Was it possible he too was going to
suffer from the family failing ?

" Do not think me cruel in asking the
question."

" I think you most cruel—most heart-
less. I cannot, will not listen to you ;"

and he rose aimlessly as though about to leave.

" Sit down, pray. Because—this is my reason for asking you—we have."

" You have what ?"

" A written statement by your son as to the girl's death."

Edward Llewellyn turned as pale as ashes. He had never felt any doubt as to the girl's fate or his son's guilt; but he faced it out before the world, and spoke of his son as a martyr to suspicion. He thought the secret, if secret there were, had died with him. Now came this ghastly resurrection. The very idea sickened him ; and yet, with an inconsistency which is by no means unusual, he stood there as if spellbound, and by his looks though not by words, begged the Dean to tell him—and for pity's sake tell him quickly—what it was he had to communicate.

What a common experience this is with us all. Some word has to be spoken, some announcement made, some letter is to come by the post, which shall be to us as the very voice of doom itself, and yet, instead of shrinking from it, we court it. We hang upon the speaker's lips, we dog the postman as he comes down the street. It is as though there were in the human breast a sort of innate pluck, an instinctive desire to know the worst, to grapple with the difficulties, and either conquer or fall in the inevitable contest.

"It is not kind to keep you in suspense. Mr. Briggs, tell Mr. Llewellyn all you know about that mysterious volume on Dovecot Hill."

Slowly and feelingly, while Edward Llewellyn listened in a perfect agony of anxiety, did Briggs communicate to him the particulars of Percy's confession.

When he had finished there was silence for some minutes; and then the Dean, rising and approaching Edward Llewellyn quite compassionately, laid his hand in a fatherly way upon his arm as he said—

"I thought it was better you should

know all this, and know it thus quietly and privately at first."

"I thank you for your consideration and delicacy, sir," replied Edward, in a broken voice, and a tone utterly unlike that which was habitual to him.

"I would not even let Mr. Alexander Lund be present; nor does he or your niece know what Mr. Briggs and myself are doing. I feel for you, deeply and truly, Mr. Llewellyn."

"Thank you, thank you!"

"And I know how terrible it would be to have all this fearful story raked up and made the subject of gossip in Zoar."

"It would kill me; or I think I should kill myself. I really do think I should follow my poor son's example, and commit suicide if this matter came out."

"As it is inevitable it shall come out if the Topaz trial goes into Court. Do you see?"

"Yes. What terms do you propose?"

"Do not put it in that way. I cannot

consent to have it go forth that we are trying to steal a march on you. I only want to get what you know I have a perfect right to get for Elsie. I do not say for Alexander Lund."

"No. Don't mention his name to me," said Edward, fiercely.

"You are wrong to be angry with him, though your wrath is comprehensible. Mr. Briggs will tell you that Alexander Lund has acted with even greater delicacy than we have done. He would not have that fatal book used in any way against you. He would not leave it in my hands lest I should use it so."

"What, you haven't got the manuscript here?"

"No; Mr. Lund retained it in his possession, but——"

"Then I don't believe a word of it. I believe it's a forgery and a swindle, if that fellow has anything to do with it. I don't mean to say," he added more calmly, "that you and Mr. Briggs are lending yourselves to this, sir; very likely even Elsie does not know the truth; but I know that fellow is perfectly capable of traducing the memory of the dead to further the ends of his ambition."

"I was with Mr. Lund when he found the book," said Briggs, quietly, "and so was the policeman. He was directed to it solely by the piece of paper found in your poor son's pocket."

"How do I know he didn't forge that as well as the book? How are we to be sure it isn't a device got up between him and the police to fix the murder on some one, and then wring the estate out of me by threats of exposure?"

"If you saw the book—saw the slip of paper—would you be satisfied?" asked the Dean. "Would you trust the evidence of your own senses, or would you think they were leagued with your enemies to deceive and wrong you?"

"Mr. Dean," said the distracted man, relapsing into his former tone, "this is a life and death matter with me, for verily I believe it will kill me if my poor son's name is bandied about in Zoar again in connexion with this horrible affair; can you wonder, then, that I require the most complete evidence, or that I suspect wherever I see a loophole for suspicion?"

"Not in the least. It is your duty to yourself and family to do so. But now tell me, supposing you identified that slip of paper and that confession as in your son's handwriting; supposing, moreover, that our theory of the will be the correct one—and you know whether that hypothesis be true or false—what would then be your course of action?"

"I scarcely know," said Edward, after a very long pause.

"It is worth considering, is it not?"

"I will consider it. Give me time to consider it."

"But then," urged the Dean, "you will consult your brother Samuel, Mr. Llewellyn, and I know—you know—what course he would suggest."

" War to the knife," said Edward.

" And he would influence you."

" He might ; yes—very likely. My own interests point in the same direction."

" Promise me, then, thus much, that you will not consult Mr. Samuel Llewellyn until you have seen us again. Let us meet here to-morrow, at this hour. We will have the paper and book ready ; you will have had time to ponder the matter. Think over it, I need not say, seriously. Think as though your dead son were by your side— perhaps he will be—as you meditate. Ask him which course he would suggest."

" I will, I will."

" May I say one word more ?"

" Yes, go on."

" Pray to Him," the old man added, very seriously, " in Whose presence both dead and living stand for guidance in this matter. Ask Him to let your poor son influence you by way of a strong impression to do what is simply right in this matter, irrespective of all other considerations. Will you do this?"

"I will."

"Think of this. We, the so-called living, and he, whom perhaps we misname dead, are not two sundered bands, as we are to the eyes of sense. We are but one company. Let us try to act in concert. Will you do this?"

"I will pray secretly this night that I may be guided to act only as I think my son would wish me."

"I ask no more. Whatever else be his fate—and I take no gloomy view of these matters—depend upon it he appraises life and all its petty incidents at their true value now."

"Then you do not think," suggested the stricken father, "that my poor son is—is lost?"

"He is in the hands of a God of mercy. Good-bye," he added, for Edward had risen to go, with pale visage and tears in his eyes. "Good-bye.   God bless and guide you."

Edward Llewellyn shambled forth from the Deanery porch in a way very different from the state of exultation he had pictured as his own if ever he should be on visiting terms with the occupant of that dignified abode. How often when our wishes are realized their very realization brings sadness where we had pictured nothing but joy!

As he emerged upon the cathedral green who should meet him—surely the strangest of all coincidences—but his sister-in-law Patty!

"Ah, Edward," she said, chirpingly. "What, paying a visit to the Deanery? Now that is mean. You should have taken Mary Ann and me with you. I like the old man, if I could only be sure his views were sound."

"I have been to the Deanery on business," Edward replied.

"And very disagreeable business, I should say, to judge by your looks. Now I cannot imagine that nice old man doing or saying anything disagreeable."

"I did not say he had."

"But you looked it. However, come and take a turn on the green."

"I can't. I have an appointment at the office."

"Those horrid appointments! Then I must walk alone."

As soon as Edward Llewellyn parted from his sister-in-law he set off, not in the direction of his office, but of the Zoar railway station, caught the omnibus going thither at a brisk pace, since it was late for the train, jumped in, remained a few minutes at the station, and came back again by the omnibus with a whole batch of passengers, who engaged him in conversation, so that he did not notice Patty plodging along on foot towards the station as he was leaving it.

When she got there, she went straight to the telegraph office, and wrote a message for Samuel Llewellyn, Gower Street, London. "Come at once. Important."

"I beg your pardon, madam," said a

smiling clerk, emerging from his den, " but is it necessary that two of these messages should be sent to Mr. Samuel Llewellyn ?"

" Two? No. Why ?"

" Because Mr. Edward Llewellyn has just been and written the same words. I was now going to wire them. Which name shall I put ?"

" Put my name, and credit me with Mr. Edward Llewellyn's payment. He evidently had forgotten that I promised to forward his message for him. Of course Mr. Samuel will come quicker for his wife than his brother, won't he ?"

" Of course, madam."

Patty was worthy to be the wife of a money-lender, so dexterously did she appropriate Edward's shilling, and so readily catch the whole bearings of the case.

So Edward had telegraphed for Sam. All was right, then. She had feared the reverse; but felt perfectly easy when she found Edward was going to call in her husband's aid.

Then came another arrival at the telegraph office. She was putting back the shilling she had saved, and meditating how a shilling saved is a shilling earned, when, in the act of depositing a stratum of tracts for purpose of safety above the rescued coin, she saw Mr. Briggs dart quickly up to the counter, and write out a telegram for Alexander Lund once more in precisely the same words as had already twice been used. "Come at once. Important." The missive, she could not help observing, was in the Dean's name.

The little clerk smiled at her when he saw her peeping over Briggs's shoulder, as much as to say, "There is a remarkable similarity in these documents, madam, is there not?"

Here was the other side marshalling its forces. There was evidently going to be an affair of some kind. How fortunate it occurred to her to follow Edward that morning. She thought he seemed absent and distrait at breakfast; noticed that he put on his walking paletôt instead of his office coat. Whither could he be going? She would see. She did, and tracked him straight to the Deanery; tarried during his somewhat protracted conversation with the Dean and Precentor, and then awaited him on the cathedral green, with what results we have seen.

She did not, of course, say a word to Edward when they met at dinner about what had occurred at the telegraph office; it would have been showing her hand too plainly, and appearing in her natural character of a female detective. She noticed that Edward was moody and dejected throughout the meal—no doubt expecting the arrival of his brother by the evening train—and that directly it was over, he retired to his private room. When tea was ready in the drawing-room he sent a servant to desire that coffee might be made for him, and sent to his sanctum, so that he could refresh himself from time to time, as he might have to work deep into the night. The ladies were on no account to sit up for him.

"What can Edward have to do that detains him so late, I wonder?" said Mary Ann.

"I know," thought Patty, though she did not say it. "He is waiting for the night mail, to see Sam."

The time for the night mail passed by and Sam did not come; but Edward Llewellyn still remained in his private room. Mary Ann retired to rest. She was one of those genteel people who take things very philosophically. Patty would give worlds to know what Edward was about. Should she go down and peep through the keyhole? Mary Ann was very deaf, and would not hear her; even if she did, Patty could pretend to be anxious about Edward. It was nothing but sisterly.

But Mary Ann was sleeping calmly, so Patty stooped at the door of Edward's room, peeped through the keyhole, and saw— what? Could she believe her eyes? Edward on his knees, praying earnestly.

She could not hear the words he said; but she caught every now and then his son's name, and the burden of his prayer seemed to be that he might be guided aright in some decision that was pressing upon him—almost that Percy might be allowed to influence him in the decision. That was as much as she could gather. How she wished Sam was here! This was the worst symptom of all. Considering what a very religious person Patty was, it seemed a strange thing for her to say, but she did say it nevertheless, that the circumstance of Edward Llewellyn praying to Heaven in the name of his dead son for guidance, was the very worst sign of all. These very religious people are not uniformly consistent. Patty was not.

When Edward had finished his prayer, he resumed what was clearly an unfinished task, and which seemed, as far as she could see from her very limited and draughty range of observation, to be some legal document. He appeared to be not merely drawing it, but actually engrossing it in clerkly fashion. He worked at it for a long time, and when he had finished it deposited it in his safe, which he locked carefully, so that there was no chance of her getting a sight of it. When he had done this, he heaved a long sigh of relief, and said as he prepared to retire—

" Thank God! I've done it."

Done what? Oh, where was Sam? Why did he not come? Edward had prayed and "done something" without Sam's connivance. This was getting serious. If Sam did not come by the first train in the morning, she must spend her saved shilling after all in another telegram.

Alec Lund duly arrived in reply to his summons, and was safely deposited at the Deanery; but Patty could not ascertain whether this was the case or not. She only dreaded lest it might be. She was quite astonished to see Edward join them the next morning at breakfast in the most genial, almost jovial frame of mind. His face had been so tragic in its grief during the prayer she had witnessed on the preceding night, that she could not account for this. True the sigh of relief came almost like an acted answer to that prayer; but she could not understand this positive exhilaration. And yet she ought to have been able to, after her long experience in T. and P. These very good people are really strange enigmas. One would think they did not quite believe even their own most cherished theories.

At the appointed hour Edward Llewellyn presented himself at the Deanery, where he found the Dean, Mr. Briggs, and Alexander Lund awaiting him. He shook hands cordially with all, but most warmly with Lund, inquiring anxiously as to Elsie's health, and not even forgetting the baby.

" Would you rather Mr. Lund left us?" asked the Dean. " He has given the—the documents to me."

" I would much rather he remained. I am glad to see him," said Mr. Llewellyn;

and such a smile passed over his face, that Alec instinctively looked round to see whether he had got Sam concealed anywhere.

"You look suspiciously at me, Alexander Lund," he continued; "and it is natural you should do so. But there is no need for you to suspect me—now. I want what I say to come very much in the way of a confession—not to you, not to any man individually. I make the confession for my own sake, simply because I think I shall feel more comfortable when I have done so."

"Honest!" ejaculated the Dean.

"Honest for a lawyer, is it not, Mr. Dean?" rejoined Edward, with the same pleasant smile. "But let me to my confession, or I may change my mind. I did after I left here yesterday. What do you think was the first thing I did when I left here?"

"What?"

"I went and telegraphed for Sam!"

"You don't mean it?" said the Dean; and Alec once more looked nervously round expecting Sam's entrance.

"Yes, I do mean it: but you needn't look for him. He's not here. He never came; so I made up my mind to act for myself."

"I'm sincerely glad to hear it," said the Dean; "and did you act on my advice?"

"Thank God! I did; and thank you for giving me the advice. Don't let's blink the matter, Mr. Dean, or you will spoil my confession. You told me to pray for guidance, and I did pray. I prayed just as you told me, that my poor dead son might be sent to influence me, to make me do what, from his new and wider plane of observation, he saw I ought to do, not what mere expediency would dictate."

"That was right," interposed the Dean.

"It was right: it is right. Let who will deride me for it by-and-by, as I know they will; but I would not exchange my present feelings for all the estates or fortunes in the world. My work last night, and my presence here this morning are the direct acted answers to prayer. What I have done and am doing is more Percy's work than mine."

They listened with the most earnest attention as he went on.

"Now, Alexander Lund, I want to deal with you first. Let me see the piece of paper you found in Percy's pocket. Let me see his diary."

Alec gave them to him—the rumpled fragment of paper taken from the dead man's person, the MS. book he had found in the nest on Dovecot Hill.

"Are they genuine?" asked the Dean.

"They are the only relics I have of the lost. Yet still I ask you, Alexander Lund, will you swear that the account you have given of these is correct?"

"I swear it solemnly."

"I do not doubt it. I could not doubt these documents," he added; "but I wanted to put the thing beyond the reach of cavil or question hereafter.   Will you give me these papers?"

Alec hesitated for a moment and looked at the Dean.

"Give them to me freely and unreservedly. You will not regret it.   You are dealing with the man now, not with the lawyer."

"Give them, by all means, Alec," said the Dean.

So Alec handed over to the father these last reminders of his unhappy son.   He put them carefully in his pocket, and drew out simultaneously another document.

"I am glad the poor fellow wrote these— glad he did all he could to make reparation for his sin before he left this world.   Perhaps I look more leniently on his act of leaving it than you clergymen, at all events, can——"

"Perhaps we are not quite so hard on these matters as you suppose," said the Dean.

"Well, be that as it may, it matters not to him.   Now, let me prove to you that he is influencing me from beyond the tomb to act in the same spirit as he acted during the last few hours of his life, to undo, as far as they can be undone, the injuries of the past. Here, Lund, I hand to you, what is really not necessary, a full and free surrender of the Topaz estate, leaving you to deal as you will by me in respect of arrears. The new house is built and furnished sumptuously. I have scarcely set foot in it, never taken possession of it; it is ready for William or you."

It may safely be averred that in the whole course of his life Alexander Lund never opened his eyes so wide as he did on this occasion.

"You stare, Alec—I may call you so now. The clerical gentlemen don't seem quite so much staggered. Perhaps it is because they do, in the exercise of their profession, occasionally catch a glimpse of the better side of human nature. I, in my business—you, in your experience, very likely see more of the bad. When I left this place yesterday, I had no more thought of preparing this deed, which I am now going to execute on William's behalf, with the Dean and Mr. Briggs for witnesses, than I had of flying over the moon. If Sam had come, I should never have done it. But I acted on your advice, Mr. Dean. I went and prayed—prayed specially that my son might sway my action, and he did. I have been but a passive instrument in this matter. I shall deliver it as my act and deed in a minute or two; but it is not so, it is Percy's. I know what it is; I see it as plainly as though it were all written down for me. He helped me in the crime, and now he helps me in undoing my misdeeds."

The instrument was duly signed and attested, in case of necessity, and to make good the title in the future. It was brief and to the point, every letter being engrossed by the hand of the man who was to execute it and strip himself, by so doing, of the greater portion of his property.

"Heaven will reward you a hundredfold for this, my dear sir," said the Dean.

"I want no reward. I've got it. I never knew what it was to feel at perfect peace before."

As Alec shook hands with his relative once more before they proceeded to join Mrs. Dean at luncheon, after repeated summonses so to do, he recited Tennyson's beautiful words—

> "'How pure at heart and sound in head,
>   With what divine affection bold,
>   Should be the man whose thought would hold
> An hour's communion with the dead!

> "'In vain shalt thou, or any, call
>   The spirits from their golden day,
>   Except, like them, thou too canst say
> My spirit is at peace with all.

> "'They haunt the silence of the breast,
>   Imaginations calm and fair,
>   The memory like a cloudless air,
> The conscience as a sea at rest.

> "'But when the heart is full of din,
>   And doubt beside the portal waits,
>   They can but listen at the gates
> And hear the household far within.'"

When Edward Llewellyn came out of the Deanery, Patty was waiting on the cathedral green as before; but seeing that Edward was leaning on the arm of Alexander Lund, and that the Dean and Mr. Briggs were in the company, and all apparently going to service, she fled precipitately.

That night she fled from Zoar, too, and without hearing the terrible news of the surrender. A letter came by the evening post from Sam's chief clerk to say her worthy husband had been, in the expressive language of the fraternity, "lagged." He had, it appeared, somewhat over-rated the idiocy of married females, and piled it on so very heavily on a certain determined lady whom he had induced to sign one of his pieces of blank paper; and the subsequent distraint upon her husband's belongings had been so very much in excess of any possible demands Mr. Samuel Llewellyn could have, that the matter had come before a police magistrate, who was so struck with

the enormity of Mr. Samuel's proceedings
that he refused to take bail for his reappearance, and Sam was in durance vile.
Hence his non-appearance at Zoar. It was
some time before any of the clerks would go
to the expense of a postage stamp on Sam's
account, or even take the trouble to write a
letter and relieve his wife's anxiety. The solicitor for the defendant, however, thought she
might be able to help him in patching up
something like a case; so Patty went back
from Zoar very crestfallen indeed, and feeling
that no amount of T. and P. would quite
reinstate the once respectable Gower Street
mansion in the esteem of the Evangelical
world.

CHAPTER VI.

WHEN Edward Llewellyn went home, and in an exhilarated way told his deaf wife what he had done in the matter of the Topaz estate, she first of all hoped she had not heard him clearly; then she made up her mind, either that he had the family failing very strongly upon him, or that he had been partaking too freely of the Dean's curious sherry for luncheon. As none of these explanations quite covered the facts, she contented herself with gazing at him as though he had been some strange extinct animal, and wondering in what direction human folly would next develop.

As for Edward Llewellyn himself, he felt no after-thrill of regret; felt only, in fact, that glow which always does follow an action done from a good conscience. When he was subsequently relieved from the fear of Sam's reappearance on the scene, and when Patty's gimlet eye was no longer near to scrutinize every movement with the minuteness of a detective policeman, he was purely at his ease, and felt the cadences of that noble excerpt from *In Memoriam* ringing in his ears, as he passed once more to the retirement of his little private office, and locking the door, prepared to hold "an hour's communion with the dead."

He drew forth from their concealment, first, the scrap of rumpled paper, which he smoothed out upon the table before him, and then the MS. volume containing the history of Percy's last days on earth. Having read this through with tearful eyes, he cleared out one of the drawers in his writing-table, and constituting this his reliquary, carefully folded up and placed within it the book and paper along with his will; in which latter he straightway entered a clause to the effect that the parcel accompanying it should be laid unopened in his coffin when he died. Thus did he make arrangements to carry his dead son's secret with him to the grave. Even Percy's mother should not know that he had confessed his guilt, or be sure that he died by his own hand.

So real and close did the presence of the dead seem to be at such times that he would scarcely have started had he heard the familiar voice break in dialogue-wise upon his train of thought. He even got into the habit of articulating his ideas, and answering in syllabled words the silent impressions that stole from time to time across his brain. Some tell us that our thoughts are always articulated. Perhaps that is one of the characteristic littlenesses of our present body of humiliation that we cannot even think without, formal though it may be, whispered words. In the more perfect corporeity the meaning may be flashed from organism to organism without this intermediate material agency.

"Who shall say," he exclaimed to himself, "that we are limited to the five senses for the impressions we receive from without? Is my communion with you, Percy, at all less perfect than that which I hold with those around me—your mother to wit?" And he smiled to think how difficult that communication was rendered by Mrs. Edward Llewellyn's exceeding deafness. Father and son had been in the habit of working so much together—whether for good or ill, it boots not to inquire now—that it seemed impossible even for death quite to break off the association. It were fanciful, perhaps, to deem that the dead did influence the living; but the living man believed it of the dead at all events; and not only so, but acted on the belief in a way contrary to the whole tenour of his previous life, and in defiance of the principles he had once adopted as his own.

Mrs. Edward Llewellyn bore the downfall of the Topaz scheme philosophically, just as she had borne her son's death, and would have borne the assurance that the end of all things was fixed for the day after to-morrow. She was one of those cold-blooded creatures who deem all sensation vulgar and are too genteel to be much interested in anybody or anything. Perhaps Edward Llewellyn might have been a better man than he had been if more happily mated. Hymen is responsible for a large number of our sins and short-comings. What a pity there is no method of re-shuffling the matrimonial cards every now and then !

There are, however, some nuptial knots which evidently require no such rearrangement. Sometimes—not often, perhaps, but occasionally—the two proper halves do get together and form one symmetrical whole. We have seen people in love with one another at their golden wedding-day; others have quarrelled like cat and dog before the honeymoon waned. It is a simple question of compatibility. They were early days with Alec Lund and his wife, to be sure; but, as far as one could see, the proper segments had collided in that case too. Even the religious difficulty did not suffice to sunder them. Elsie bore the announcement of her good fortune quite as philosophically as Mrs. Edward did the news of the reverse. Perhaps she eyed Plantagenet somewhat more proudly as the heir-apparent, and was glad to think her husband need not feel forced to work at anything uncongenial for the future. What with Aunt Phillis's money, his own small income, and now with the Topaz rents, they were really "well off" for young folks; and the first result was that Amy was declared to be "finished," and Elsie centred all her attention on her liege lord and their united offspring.

"You are a most phlegmatic person, Mrs. Lund, ain't you?" said Mrs. Fane, a few days after Elsie's good fortune had become known.

"A regular Dutchwoman, yes; but what makes you say so now?"

"I fully expected you would put on a

crimson velvet turban or a sky-blue satin gown for breakfast, or at least array Plantagenet in amber silk, to mark your accession to wealth. I should have done something outrageous, I know."

" I want to do something outrageous too. Will you help me ?"

" With all my heart. Which is it, the crimson turban, the sky-blue satin, or the amber silk ?"

" Neither. I want you and Amy to come down with us when we go to take possession."

" Don't talk like a bailiff."

" I really feel like one, going and sitting down in chairs I haven't bought, and sleeping on beds chosen by somebody else. But will you come ?"

" Willingly ; though the proceeding is not outrageous enough for me. Let us hire the triumphal car from one of the travelling circuses and enter the town drawn by sixteen cream-coloured horses."

" That is a practical detail we can

arrange afterwards. Will you come, that's all?"

"I will. We shall certainly want a special train, for Mr. and Mrs. William Llewellyn are going, are they not?"

"Yes; I mentioned the result to my father, and asked him what he would like to do, whether he would turn squire and take Topaz—for it is his, remember, not ours—we shall be only there on sufferance."

"I know. What did he choose?"

"To have the old High Street house changed from a shop to a private dwelling, and there vegetate the rest of his days."

"And a much more sensible plan than I should have given your good father credit for. It's a wonder he didn't want to fit it up as a shrine for Moddle."

"He tells me you speak of Mr. Moddle as 'Tommy' in private. Is that true?"

"Very true, of course."

"But you *do* like him, don't you?"

"Vastly."

" No, but really ?"

" Will you oblige me by talking of something or somebody else ?"

" Oh !" said Elsie, significantly, " I understand. I want no other information. Moddle, I see, must be contemplated in any family arrangements."

But Mrs. Fane said nothing.

Some little time elapsed before the exodus could be made; and in the meanwhile vast changes took place at Zoar, affecting indirectly some of the personages in our history.

The Right Reverend Father in God John Lord Bishop of Zoar, after a lengthened career of general inutility, departed from this sublunary sphere, to reap, it is to be hoped, something more than the result of his earthly labours. Who was to be his successor ?

Many were the throbbing hearts among the parsonic protégés of the Government both in and out of the diocese; for it was not supposed that there would be a translation in this instance. There were ex-college fellows by the score, who had qualified by editing the Greek Tragedians, schoolmasters who had caned little boys, and Heads of Colleges who had rusticated refractory Undergrads—all were pining for the otium cum dignitate of Zoar Palace, and egging on their friends to put in a word with the Premier for their elevation to the apostolate. It seemed a roundabout way of doing things when one came to think of it; but a State Church is of necessity a complicated piece of machinery, and the prevailing custom, if it did nothing else, ballasted the old boat and prevented her from riding too nautilus-like over the waves of society. But tragic editors, fierce schoolmasters, fiery Heads of Houses, and all the race of ex-fellows and aspiring incumbents were doomed to disappointment. A rare precedent was followed of exalting the Dean to the bishopric of his diocese. Our very reverend friend simply went over the way from the Deanery to the Palace, and became our Right Reverend Father in God forthwith.

This led to other mutations, and a general move-up ensued. Canon Wilcox of St. Hilda's was elevated to the deanery, retaining his incumbency, and our good friend Briggs was made a full-blown canon, being about the most juvenile dignitary in the *Clergy List*. Such a thoroughly domestic series of changes had seldom been known. No new element was introduced. It was doubtful whether Briggs's precentor-ship would be filled up for the present, as he would be on the spot still to manage the music. The beneficed clergy in and out of the diocese, ex-fellows, schoolmasters and Heads of Colleges were wild for the space of a week, and wrote letters to the daily papers, wherein the words jobbery and corruption were of frequent occurrence.

"What a pity you are not in orders, Lund," wrote the Bishop-elect. " You could have walked into Briggs's minor canonry, with St. Simon Magus' to boot.

Be my first candidate for orders, do, my dear Alexander. I can't allow Briggs to hold St. Simon Magus' permanently with his canonry. It would be starting him too soon as a pluralist. Recant your Popish errors, Lund, let me receive you and ordain you. The preferment shall await your readiness to accept it."

With many thanks Alec said he would take time to think of the proposal, and discuss it verbally when they met. It was no secret that he had not found all he expected on the other side of the Rubicon; but those who knew him best doubted very much whether he would ever bring his mind to suggest or sanction his recrossing it.

At length the migration took place, and a jovial party it was that assembled in the little city. The only feature of the progress which at all came up to Mrs. Fane's idea of propriety was that the cathedral bells were rung by order of the Bishop to celebrate the event. Not that they heard much of them except in the far distance, for they skirted the actual city, and all assembled at Topaz.

"I consider this slow," said the volatile widow. "I should have had the sixteen cream-coloured steeds and a band of music. What say you, Mr. William Llewellyn?"

"I am thinking how very much in the position of Jacob on the occasion of his family going down to Egypt I myself am to-day."

"Enlighten me. I never was great at Old Testament history."

"Jacob in Goshen played such a thorough second fiddle to Joseph; and so too, Lund is assuming the Squire, while I am to retire to my humble roof in the High Street."

"Lund is your tenant-at-will at Topaz, and you can turn him out whenever you feel squire-like. There you have the advantage over Jacob."

"True."

At the entrance of Topaz stood Edward

Llewellyn—minus his deaf wife, it was
noticed—ready to receive them and instal
them in their new abode.   On his face was
the smile of a man who not only feels he
had done his duty, but is conscious of
escape from the greater of two evils in
doing so.   Edward Llewellyn's conduct
seemed quite angelic, and was so spoken of
among his neighbours and kinsmen; but
he had really done a very good stroke of
business too.   He had escaped the odium
and expense of a lawsuit in which he would
certainly have been worsted, even if the
facts which came out did not bring him
within reach of the criminal law.   Instead
of being saddled with years upon years of
arrears, he squared all that by handing over
the Topaz mansion—which he must have
done in any case if worsted—and the household furniture; and really those effects,
massive and costly as they were, slenderly
represented the accumulations of the Topaz
rents which he would have had to disgorge.
The plain English of the arrangement was

that William Llewellyn had let his brother off very easily, and Edward had made a much better arrangement than as though he had taken Sam's advice and fought to the death. Poor Sam was a prisoner of war in another of these unsuccessful campaigns against circumstances.

And then Edward had got all the honour and glory too, and exactly the honour and glory he wanted. There it stood embodied in the august forms of the Right Reverend the Bishop, the Very Reverend the Dean of Zoar, and the Reverend Canon Briggs. Mr. Edward Llewellyn was literally fraternizing with them as a man and a brother. Hitherto his fraternization had been of a very far-off kind, but this coup had made him one with all that saintly circle. When the new arrivals had descended from their carriages, Edward pointedly shook hands with his brother William first, and formally installed him as lord of Topaz. This was a concession to propriety in which he was followed by the three august guests, and then Alec and Elsie came in for their share of the congratulations. The very baby was fêted as future successor. There were, in fact, three generations of the lords of Topaz represented on the occasion.

"It strikes me," said Mrs. Fane, to Mrs. William Llewellyn and Amy, "that we may as well retire to our rooms or take a walk in the grounds; we seem to be de trop."

With manifold apologies, Alec Lund did the work of introduction; and, in a few minutes, everybody knew everybody else. There was no necessity, and no chance, of the charming widow beating a retreat, for straightway there began an active contest between the dignitaries who should secure her for a tête-à-tête on the lawn before dinner. The Bishop and Dean of course carried off the palm, and divided the honours. Briggs—we beg his pardon, Canon Briggs—was obliged to pair off with Amy, and went, with a by no means martyr-like air, to inspect the rosary in her company.

All the guests remained to dinner. It had been planned as a pleasant surprise by Edward Llewellyn that the house-warming should take place on the very day when the hosts arrived. There was some little discussion as to who should occupy the post of honour at dinner; but Mr. William Llewellyn was so very decided in his refusal, and his "estimable wife," as he always termed her, was so exceedingly. averse to anything like prominence, that Alec and Elsie adorned the ends of the table—an oval one, by the way, which did much to remove the difficulty, and rub off all corners, as the Bishop said. By the time Plantagenet was brought in to dessert, the young host and hostess felt as much at home as in their suburban villa, and seemed to have been the lord and lady of Topaz all their lives. If you or I, good reader, were elevated to a position of eminence, in proportion to that we now occupy, to-morrow, we should—always assuming that we are philosophers—be as much at home in it the day after as though to the manner born.

The cup of Edward Llewellyn's joy was full; no dreg of bitter remaining. The Bishop and Dean in the post-prandial exuberance of their hearts promised to dine on an early day beneath his roof; engaging in the meantime that the ladies should exchange something more than pasteboards, and hoping Mr. and Mrs. Edward Llewellyn would favour them with their company at the Palace and Deanery on certain days then and there named. Virtue was triumphant where intrigue and finesse had failed to carry their points.

"Briggs and I—it is as difficult to call him Canon as for him to address me as ' my lord'—are coming to see you to-morrow, Lund," said the Bishop, as they left, late in the evening. " Think over the subject of my last letter, will you? What Briggs wants I have no idea—or only a vague one

—but he insists on accompanying me. I told him he would be in the way."

"I shall be delighted to have a conversation with you, my lord—I can say it naturally, you see—and we will get Mrs. Fane and Amy to take care of Briggs."

Why should Amy blush so, and Briggs look so wonderfully sly at this very simple and natural arrangement?

When Alec and Elsie retired after this first day of their strange new lives, instead of dwelling on the happiness of their metamorphosis, or even acknowledging the care and consideration with which Edward Llewellyn had fitted up Alec's little dressing-room as a second study, the two young people sat down in this sanctum and indulged in a very long and elaborate theological argument. Though theological, however, it had no element of discord in it, and never on any occasion approached the limits of a curtain lecture, though it was carried on to the very last moment before they closed their eyes. Perhaps the reason of this was that the lady carried her point, and the husband confessed that his recent action had been precipitate.

It does so simplify matrimonial discussion when the wife is altogether triumphant and the husband purely concessive.

The next afternoon his lordship and Briggs arrived in due course, and the young canon was, after a short interval, marshalled to the drawing-room, and handed over to the custody of the ladies.

"Now, my very good friend, Alexander Lund," began the Bishop, posing himself as episcopally as he could in the capacious easy chair which was provided for Alec's meditations or siestas, "have you, as I proposed, reconsidered your position ? Have you decided to accept my offer ?"

"Tell me, my lord, would you not rather despise me if I said 'yes?'"

"Would you oblige me, just for the period of our present interview, by dropping that expression 'my lord'? Perhaps for a little while afterwards, until my ear grows accustomed to it, I should be glad for you to resume it. But just now I am very anxious that both you and I should forget the fact of my being a bishop, and should talk as man and man—as two old friends."

"Thank you very much. Would you not despise me if, allured by your very tempting offers, I repudiated vows which I had deliberately taken upon myself?"

"Yes, I certainly should."

"Yet you urge such a course."

"I do not."

"How so?"

"I demur to the assertion that you would change through the airy allurements I could offer—not only your previous character, but your present position does away with any such idea. I still more emphatically deny that you made your recent choice deliberately. You did it on impulse, and without due consideration."

"Who says so?"

"Mrs. Fane. She pleads guilty to having prompted you; and — between ourselves,

don't mention it to my wife—I can quite
understand that most fascinating widow
landing a helpless fellow anywhere."

" And she actually pleads guilty?"

" Yes.   In answer to what I confess was
a leading question, she rather thought she
had succeeded in making a very bad
Romanist out of a respectably good Anglican."

" What a confession!"

" She is too good and genuine not to
acknowledge an error."

"And what does she—what do you—
suggest that I should do?"

" Re-'vert.   That is the proper phrase, is
it not?"

" I believe so.   And the world will say I
did it for filthy lucre's sake."

" Where is your world?   Is it not here?
Are they—are we—likely to say or think so?
Supposing all the world outside sufficiently
interested in you to say or think such a
thing, what then?"

" Let them rave, you would say."

" Yes, but ask yourself—would they rave ?
If I guess rightly, the world in which you
feel interest next to the world of home is
the literary world. Tell me, do you think
your press friends would rave at your re-
version ?"

" With joy, yes."

" Exactly. But, after all, the matter is
one between your own conscience and God.
Have you settled it there, Lund ?"

" Between my own conscience and my
wife—who seems to me and to you, I know,
very often to speak words beyond her own
on these matters—I have settled it."

" And your decision there ? By the way,
where is Elsie ? Why is she not here ?
Would you mind ringing for her ?"

Alec gave a triple ring, which in the old
home had always been the signal that he
wanted his wife to join him in his sanctum.
Elsie was by his side in a moment.

" Hither she comes, like a good fairy.
Now, Elsie dear," continued the old man,
" come and coil yourself up on this foot-

stool as you used to when we read the
Ethics at the Deanery. I want your husband—as he has told you—to re-'vert. I
want him to take orders. I want him to be
incumbent of St. Simon Magus. I should
greatly like him to be my examining
chaplain when he is a little older. And
if he can sing, the Dean will, in the interim,
promote him to Briggs's minor canonry.
Do I bait temptingly?"

"Too temptingly. Alec fears his return
to the Church of England will be mis-
interpreted."

"Then let him return without any
definite understanding at all. I make no
promises. Bishops have lots of applications,
and sometimes short memories. Come back,
you interesting prodigal, and leave the
fatted calf to be killed or not, and the music
and dancing to be provided or omitted as
circumstances may dictate."

"Under those conditions he shall come
back. I promise for him."

"Then I ask him no more about the

matter. You are so very much his better half."

Although not given to the melting mood, as is the custom of her sex, and very much, under ordinary contingencies, the reverse of demonstrative, Elsie Lund shed happy tears when she saw Alec thus silently yield. She had felt, far more acutely than she cared to confess, the little rift within the lute which was caused by his hasty step. At the same time, had she seen him really happy in the new faith he had chosen, she would have followed him, even against her better judgment, having such implicit trust that what satisfied him would content her too. But she saw he was not at home. She knew this retrograde step would one day have to be taken. Could it have come more opportunely than now at the commencement of their new life, when fortune had begun to smile upon them? One only possible addition to her present happiness remained, and that depended on Alec feeling himself able to accept the position the Bishop offered him.

About this, however, there was ample time for discussion.

They talked long and pleasantly over the past and present, and even sent long glances forward into the future. The Bishop was in a humour to be pleased with everything ; but especially lauded Edward Llewellyn to the skies. His concession was, he said, a pure piece of nineteenth century Christianity, none the worse because it comprised a large ingredient of the serpent's wisdom. His taste in domestic architecture and adornment was exquisite. Topaz was a model of a country gentleman's—should he say a suburban incumbent's ?—house.

While they were engaged in these pleasant colloquies the minutes and hours passed rapidly away, and poor Canon Briggs was quite forgotten. At last a timid knock was heard at the study door, and everybody simultaneously remembered his existence, and pronounced his name under their breath.

" Come in," shouted Alec.

It was not Briggs. It was Mrs. Fane, who opened the door and stood statue-like just inside with a face of woe.

"Something dreadful has happened," she said, in answer to the mute appeal of all three.

"In the name of pity, what?" said Elsie, of course thinking, mother-like, of her baby.

"No; it's not Plantagenet. It's nothing affecting any of you. Something dreadful has happened to me."

"My dear friend, what?" asked Elsie.

"Ah! you bear it much more calmly now."

"What is it?" asked her two male sympathizers.

"Something so horrible and heartrending that I cannot frame my lips to tell you. Come in, please," she said to somebody outside.

Canon Briggs and Amy came in at her bidding, looking very sheepish; the gentleman, if it must be confessed, much more so than the lady.

The Bishop only looked sly; but Alec Lund gave speech to his thoughts and said—

"Oh! I think I understand the catastrophe."

"Pardon me," answered Mrs. Fane, "I don't think you do. You jump to conclusions. I complain to you, Mr. Lund, in your capacity of host, to you, my lord, as Bishop of the diocese, in reference to this person whom you have allowed to associate with my daughter."

"Briggs?" said the Bishop, really beginning to be mystified. "What has he done?"

"Taken advantage of Mr. Lund's hospitality, and that girl's guileless unsuspecting nature, to argue against her faith and mine."

"What, Briggs been proselytizing?"

"He has, and what is more, he has succeeded."

"In converting your daughter?"

"No; in *per*-verting her."

"I have *re*-verted, my lord," said Amy, with the most wicked sniggle.

"So somebody else has been at that game besides myself," exclaimed Alec Lund; "and pray what bribe did he offer you to get you back, Amy?"

Amy hung her head; and Canon Briggs was obliged to speak.

"I cannot look upon it as a bribe; but 1 asked this lady to be my wife."

"Sudden," said the Bishop.

"Indecently so," added Mrs. Fane.

"You don't either of you think so," said Alec Lund. "We could tell them a thing or two about that, could we not, Elsie?"

"Perhaps."

"There is an old proverb about marrying in haste and repenting at leisure," suggested the Bishop, sententiously.

"That is just what we want Mrs. Fane to let us do," said Briggs. "If she will consent to our marrying in haste, we will take our leisure in repenting."

"Prettily put, Briggs. I never knew you

were a ladies' man before.   How say you,
Mrs. Fane ?"

" As a lone lorn widow is it fair I should
be subjected to this kind of thing ?   What
can I say ?"

" It's her way of saying ' Yes,' " observed
Alec.   " She never does it in a monosyllable."

" Hold your tongue, you renegade."

" I shan't.   I feel so extremely happy to
think that, whereas you bagged Amy and
me at one feel swoop, and without either of
us knowing in the least what we were
about, so now you have lost us simultaneously and without your knowing what
we were about."

" And now I suppose you think you will
get *me* back too."

" On the contrary," answered Alec.   " In
all sincerity and seriousness I believe the
Roman system is made for you and you for
the Roman system.   I should be sorry to
see you come back."

" Is that meant for a compliment to me
or to my faith ?"

"To both. Only it is something more than a compliment. It means that you are admirably suited to one another."

"Thank you."

"Welcome."

"You haven't got a nice heretical Canon or anything you could recommend me, have you, Elsie?"

"Oh no. You are bespoken."

"What do you mean?"

"Tommy."

"Don't be ridiculous."

The time passed away pleasantly enough in settling down into the new home, and watching the billing and cooing of the young couple. Mrs. Fane's visit was prolonged sine die, and it was at length decided that she should not return until after Amy's marriage.

"It is entirely preposterous to talk of that immature creature being married," said her mamma. "Plantagenet is quite as capable of appreciating the duties and obligations of marriage.

Alec Lund had now realized what he considered the acme of existence. He could indulge his literary tastes when and how he liked. He could write for fame—if at all—not for money; and he soon found himself really more prolific than in old times, when he was obliged to force his intellect or his inclinations. Just as there are no people so busy as idle ones, so very often there are no people who waste so much time as those who pretend to be always preternaturally busy.

His mornings he passed in his study, and his afternoons were often devoted to arrangements about his bijou estate. There was quite enough to keep him employed without the danger of making existence merely bucolic. The dinner-hour brought social converse at home or abroad. He had just as much society as he wanted, and of the kind he liked. The Palace, the Deanery, and the canons' houses were the places of reunion, and at each and all Edward Llewellyn and his wife were constant guests, while they amply returned the hospitality, and their house was numbered among the centres of cathedral society.

High Street, however, was the most remarkable phenomenon in this way that Zoar had ever witnessed. It formed a neutral territory on which the grandees and the bourgeois might meet. Hitherto the line had been sharply drawn between what it was really no hyperbole to term the two castes. Now the old house was a horizon on which the two worlds—the social sky and sea—blended imperceptibly.

"This is a change, mother, isn't it?" said Mr. William Llewellyn, sitting down, after the initiatory festivities were over, in the large dining-room which occupied the space formerly covered by the shop.

"A blessed change, indeed. I feel as though I had come back to this dear old place—the scene of our former troubles—to die."

"Well, that's a cheerful view to take of matters, anyhow."

"It is no sad one in my estimation. We are old people now, and our time cannot be far off. We shall not be long separated, whichever goes first. Now that our dear Elsie is settled so happily, what else is there to live for here?"

As if to answer that question, Elsie's baby, who was out for a perambulator-ride, was wheeled up to the window where they were sitting.

"Baby comes to rebuke you," said Mr. Llewellyn, carrying on at the window in that idiotic manner which is supposed to be peculiarly interesting to infant faculties, but which that particular infant treated with the most profound disdain.

Then Alec and Elsie came in, and the baby was retained for a long evening. It seemed really as if the old times were coming back with a difference, but a difference altogether in the right direction.

"Your mother has been treating us to an original version of the *Nunc Dimittis*, Elsie," said Mr. Llewellyn."

"Until I was very properly reminded that I have something to live for still in this dear child."

"This child," said its mamma, "runs considerable risk of growing up the most detestable pet lamb that ever butted at its benefactors. What a delicate compliment to the rest of your family, mother, to say that you only want to live for this most insignificant fragment of humanity, who is quite unable to appreciate your compliment, and is, moreover, excellently cared for by his nurse and mother."

"I was only saying that I felt I had come back here to die—it may be years hence; and your father must needs take it up and make a fuss."

"You spoke to me as though you were on the point of ordering your funeral."

"My dear mother is going to be one of the most regular of my congregation," said Alec Lund.

"Your congregation?" said Mrs. Llewellyn.

"My congregation at St. Simon Magus'. Yes, I have come round to the Bishop's way of thinking at last. I feel what I believe to be an honest call to take orders. The Bishop wishes it, dear Elsie wishes it, and now I wish it myself."

"It will be my greatest comfort and happiness," said Mrs. Llewellyn.

"It's the right thing, I'm sure," added Mr. Llewellyn.

"And yet do you remember what a bad character I once had in Zoar? I believe you all shared it, except this dear long-legged creature," meaning his wife.

"Please don't revive that ancient heresy about my legs, or I shall fancy all your bad character is coming back again."

"I like you, of all people in the world, twitting me with my bad character. Why, about the only erratic thing I ever did in my life you helped me to do."

"And that was——"

"Carry on with you while you were engaged to Percy. Really my conscience doesn't smite me with anything else."

"And it's pretty easy on that score, too, I think."

"Yes, it doesn't hurt much. But it is remarkable how easily some men, especially if they are careless about the conventionalities of life, get a character for being rakes and everything that is dreadful. Few men have led a quieter life than myself. I have thought freely; but my freedom has never led me into loose living. On the contrary, knowing that my faith—or my absence of faith—might be ill-spoken of through my frailties, I was particularly careful not to give occasion to the enemy to blaspheme."

"May I ask you," said Mr. William Llewellyn, with a roguish twinkle of the eye, "what particular form of faith you profess just at present?"

"There is a strong temptation to retort on you with a *tu quoque*, and ask what particular form of faith *you* profess; but I refrain, and candidly tell you that, at this moment, I am bound to no special form."

"The best religion of all," said Mrs. Llewellyn.

"Perhaps so ; but, mother, I am a weak vessel, and require some form, and I shall adopt the Church of England pure and simple as the one which combines in the most perfect harmony, faith, and reason, the wisdom of the serpent, and the harmlessness of the dove."

"And the ministry of which you are the very man to adorn, dear Alec."

"Thank you, mother. I value such spontaneous testimony far beyond that of a whole bench of bishops."

So the time wore on, and once more the golden summer deepened into autumn, Zoar's most beautiful season. Among its russet woods and over the very field-paths along which Alec and Elsie used to take their stolen walks, Briggs and Amy now wandered, with none to say them nay, beguiling the time until the waning year

should bring around their nuptial day.
Briggs, once the most unromantic of his
race, had become softened by the presence
of his beautiful fiancée; and never did his
clear voice ring out so silvery among the
cathedral aisles as since Amy had crossed
his once lonely path. The little house in
the Vicars' Close, where once had been his
lodging, fell vacant opportunely, and was
now to be their home. It would suffice at
first until they should see their way to en-
tering on the ampler accommodation of the
canon's residence, which Briggs was now
glad to let furnished to a wealthy visitor.
That dear old cathedral which had been so
greatly the means of bringing them all
together from the first, was marked by
quite a succession of events during the re-
mainder of that year in connexion with the
different personages in this story.

First of all, Alec was determined to mark
his recurrence to his old faith in a quasi-
public manner. He would not, as he
phrased it, sneak back into the Church of

England as though he were ashamed of it. So one Sunday afternoon, much to the amazement of the ordinary worshippers, and greatly to the edification of the theological students, Alec knelt before the altar, and was formally received by the Bishop of Zoar once more into communion with the Church of England.

Father Pugin wrote a kind letter congratulating him on having seen his way clear for returning, and promising to pay him a visit, and assist at another ceremony which he had heard was not far off. He fulfilled that promise, and was one of those who laid his hands along with the Bishop, the Dean and Canon Briggs on the head of the Reverend Alexander Lund, who was ordained deacon in the Cathedral Church of St. Andrew Zoar, and was to share, during the year of his diaconate, the ministry of St. Simon Magus', with the Reverend Canon Briggs.

The marriage of that same Canon Briggs and Amy Fane was deferred until after the ordination, because it was held to be absolutely essential that Alec Lund should assist the Bishop at that ceremony. Briggs did not feel sentimental on that score—men seldom do ; but Amy was resolved that she would have the exhortation read to her by Alec Lund, or not be married at all.

The marriage took place from Topaz, and was about the gayest thing of the kind that had ever been witnessed in the old cathedral within the memory of the most ancient inhabitant. Pugin remained for that too ; in fact it seemed as if everybody who came to Topaz stopped there, and forgot his or her ordinary duties to society from that time forth.

" Mrs. Fane," said Father Pugin, at the wedding breakfast, " don't you find this kind of thing catching ?"

" Meaning the marrying ?"

" Yes."

" Very. And you ?"

" If my vows of celibacy did not stand in the way, I should propose on the spot."

" To me, of course ?"

"To whom else?"

"Not the slightest use, Father Pugin," said Lund, "she's bespoken."

"Indeed, by whom?"

"Tommy."

"Which Tommy?"

"Moddle."

"Don't believe it. What do you say, Mrs. Fane?" And really Father Pugin looked so languishing, that there is no knowing what might not have happened if those dreadful vows of celibacy had not stood in the way.

"Propose and try," said the volatile widow.

"A fair challenge!" said Lund. "Now silence, please; Father Pugin is going to propose."

"I do propose," he said, "I am privileged 'for old acquaintance' sake to propose —the health of the bride and bridegroom."

So he made the accustomed speech on the occasion, and did not respond to the very determined challenge of his fair assailant.

The wedding had taken place in the cathedral—the last in the links of those events which served to endear the old place for long years in the memories of those present. At the marriage the Communion had been administered to the bride and bridegroom; and now another departure was made from ordinary custom. After the wedding breakfast the whole party adjourned to afternoon service in the cathedral, and the bride and bridegroom departed thence for their wedding tour. Considering the close association of the bridegroom with the cathedral such an arrangement was most appropriate.

It was only when they were saying good-bye at the western door that it transpired they were going to Wales for their tour. Briggs's friends belonged to the Principality; and Alec and Elsie half promised —Plantagenet permitting—to run down and join them towards the close of their honeymoon, and thus have a final search for their Mudwalla estate.

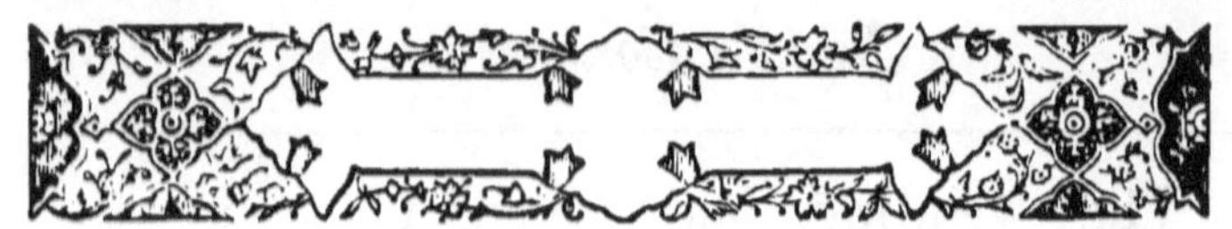

CHPTER VII.

PASTOR ANGLICANUS.

NO sooner had the Reverend Alexander and Mrs. Lund settled down comfortably in their luxurious home at Topaz than they immediately proceeded to illustrate two time-honoured adages. The first was that man, as at present constituted, is not capable of rest. He longs for it, and, as soon as he attains it, finds it irksome. The second was that, if you still judge him by his unstudied acts rather than his formal words and studied professions, the more man has the more he wants.

Alec Lund's life in London had been a laborious one. None is more so than that of descriptive writer on a daily paper. The life of the leader-writer pure and simple is exacting in an intellectual sense, but demands no physical exertion. The outside graphic writer—a creation of the present era of journalism—involves work of muscle as well as brain. Besides, he did his full share of leader-writing and reviewing, but never made either of these his speciality. Suddenly he settled down to wealth and tranquillity at Zoar. At first it seemed to him perpetual holiday. Anon he exaggerated his occupations and fancied himself busy; and no sooner was he actually in orders than he discovered he wanted a holiday. Elsie found out at the same time that she had been devoting herself too exclusively to Plantagenet; and so the arrangement was made with Briggs and Amy that the four should meet in Wales when the honeymoon was waning, and the autumnal moon simultaneously shone in the literal heavens.

Then again the locality which Briggs had chosen for his marriage trip proved very attractive to Alec Lund. The Mudwalla estates lay somewhere in Wales; so

much had been ascertained. Why should
they not devote the holiday to hunting up
their lost inheritance? When they only
had the suburban house, and their income
was limited to the earnings of Alec on the
press and of Elsie as a daily governess, they
talked often and often of dropping their
claim to Topaz and thinking no more of
Mudwalla. Now Topaz had come to them
almost unsought they suddenly discovered
that they wanted Mudwalla too. At all
events it could do no harm to look it up,
they thought. If it really turned out to be
nothing more than a figment of poor Aunt
Rachel's brain, the sooner it was disposed of
in that category the better.

This was Edward Llewellyn's idea. He
asserted—and his testimony seemed above
suspicion now—that he had no idea of the
substantial existence of Mudwalla. "You
know, Lund," he said, "I was sharp enough
a little while since in finding out anything
that would bring money. We scoured
Wales over——"

" Who ?"

" Poor Percy and myself; and Sam was mostly there when he was supposed to be evangelizing; but not a trace of the lost estate could we find."

" Perhaps the very anxiety of the search prevented you from discovering it. I have heard that if you are benighted when on horseback, and lose your way, the best plan is simply to drop your rein on the horse's neck and let him drift."

" True, I've done it over and over again myself."

" And came right?"

" Always."

" That's exactly what Elsie and I will do, then. I'll get somebody to take my work for a month, and we'll drift all over Wales. I'll wager we come upon Mudwalla if it exists."

" It does *not* exist," said Edward, dog-matically.

On the other hand, William felt quite sure it did exist, and believed Alec would find it by some such method as he purposed. He himself was anxious that a clairvoyant should be tried. "Indeed," he said, "you young folks seem to forget that it's *my* estate again you are looking for; and therefore I think I ought to be allowed to hunt for it after my own fashion."

"By all means, you hunt in your way; we in ours."

"But there are no mediums in Zoar."

"Send a lock of your hair—with a remittance, of course—to some medium in London and you will get something, no doubt."

There is little doubt that Mr. William Llewellyn did send as purposed, and got something in return; but it never transpired what it was. He was seldom known to mention a medium again, however; and rather fought shy of the subject of clairvoyance.

Almost before the Welsh expedition was finally decided upon, imploring letters came from Canon and Mrs. Briggs, begging them on no account to abandon the idea. The newly-married couple were, of course, as happy as the days were long (the days, by the way, were beginning to " draw in"), but still they would like to see their old friends. They talked, or rather wrote, as though they had been away for years. We have known cases where, under conditions of perfect happiness, the honeymoon thus palled. Man cannot realize unadulterated bliss here below. Too much honey surfeits. The moon blinds by excess of light.

So Alec and his wife went. Plantagenet was committed to the care of his grand-mamma, who took up her quarters at Topaz for the purpose; but Mrs. Fane was also promoted to the post of secretary in that infantile household. No baby born in the purple could have been more elaborately cared for. Was he not heir of Topaz, and possibly of Mudwalla?

The Briggses and Lunds met at a border town, resolved to hunt the Principality high and low for the lost inheritance.

"We'll stop here one night, and then open 'Bradshaw' 'promiscuously,' as they say, and drift," said Alec.

"The very thing," replied Briggs. "Now come and dine. I cannot tell you what a relief it will be to see other faces than that beautiful one of Amy's around my table."

"Ingrate!"

"Not at all. But did you not find something of the same kind when you were first made inexpressibly happy?"

"You forget our marriage was a Bohemian one. It's only your prim conventional affairs that entail this period of segregation from the rest of humankind. Why should not people go out and get married in the morning, and come back as though nothing had happened?"

"But something has happened."

"Yes, but nothing to go into voluntary exile about, that I can see."

"Ah, you're a practical man."

"Thank Heaven I am."

The dinner was a merry one; and, when

it was over, as a fraction of daylight still remained due, it was proposed that they should take a walk and study an autumn sunset effect.

The two young matrons walked together, and soon got far ahead of their lords and masters, who were smoking their cigars and sauntering as became church dignitaries in mufti.

They soon got out of the little town, and mounting a height looked down on a perfect panorama of valley scenery, bounded by hills which almost attained the dignity of mountains in the far west. Behind these the sun was setting, and threw into prominence what appeared to be a splendid castellated mansion on the summit of a slight eminence, between those farther elevations and that on which the gazers were standing. The structure had evidently caught the fancy of the two ladies, and they stopped a peasant presumably for the purpose of inquiry about it; for he pointed to it, and talked volubly to them. No sooner had he commenced his discourse than Elsie flew off as fast as her long legs would carry her, and rushing up to her husband said, with spent breath—

"Alec, what *do* you think that place is?"

"That Brummagem castle yonder?"

"Yes."

"I should think, by your excitement, it could be none other than Mudwalla."

"It *is* Mudwalla!"

They had drifted right by a miracle. Their very first footfall in the Principality had landed them at the very place they had so long been seeking in vain. Previous searchers had never thought of stopping short at the border, but penetrated far into Wales before they began to hunt. Besides this, they had jumped to the conclusion that Mudwalla was the phonetic mode of representing some unpronounceable name of a Welsh village. Mudwalla was the real name; a sham Welsh appellation coined by some would-be Welshman, of a previous generation, and still perpetuated by the present owner, who—the peasant informed them—was a wealthy gentleman from London, grown rich by the pursuit of soap-boiling. The aborigine was well posted up in the previous history of the place, and told them, what Aunt Rachel probably did not know, that Lloyd Llewellyn and Susanna Dash both sold their estates when they left Wales to the family from whom it passed to the present owner.

This was a rude disruption of their day-dreams. It would have been bad enough to feel sure, as they did, that their castle was a Spanish one; but to know that it was Brummagem and owned by a soap-boiler was dreadful in the extreme.

The next morning Briggs and Alec called on the only solicitor in the town, who, of course, was man of business for Mr. Jones of Mudwalla—the soap-boiler's name was so far Welsh, at all events. They told him plainly the nature of their quest, and the little man entered into the spirit of the thing, and showed them the title-deeds.

His progenitor had managed the sale for Mrs. Dash and Lloyd Llewellyn; and not only so, but purchased for the lady the Topaz estate at Zoar with the proceeds of her sale, less a certain portion (not to be named, even now), which went to relieve the difficulties of her fickle neighbour and former lover.

"So Topaz *is* Mudwalla, my dear, you see," said Alec.

"And we have recovered our Welsh estates; let us rest and be thankful."

"You may say so, madam," replied the little Welsh lawyer, appearing to enjoy the joke. "Topaz is Mudwalla metamorphosed. I wish you all joy in your possession of it."

"The most marvellous part of all this strange adventure," said Alec, as they returned to their hotel, "is that diminutive lawyer."

"Why?"

"He refused a fee!"

"How Sam would despise him," said Elsie.

"Talk of a certain person, and he will appear," exclaimed Briggs, as they entered the private sitting-room of the hotel.

" What, has Sam hove in sight?"

" No; but here's his trial, in the London papers; and by all that's Evangelical," added the youthful Canon, " Patty is in the same boat with him !"

" What?"

"True. The pair are indicted for conspiring to extort money."

" And that T. and P. should come to this! Do read," said Elsie.

So Briggs read the account of Sam's final escapade. He had chosen for his victim a schoolmaster in difficulties, or rather victimized the schoolmaster's wife, who tried the forlorn hope of getting her lord and master out of his trouble by the expedient of money borrowed at sixty per cent. Sam got this lady to put her husband's name to bills, and then threatened her with being prosecuted for forgery unless she complied with his extortionate demands.

"What a nice old gentleman!" exclaimed Amy.

"There are lots of them about," remarked Alec.

"But the lady," Briggs continued, "made a clean breast of it to her lord and master, who, of course, said she had authority to sign cheques, and therefore the fact of her putting his name to acceptances was only an error of judgment."

"But how was poor Patty brought in?" Elsie asked.

"Patty persuaded the lady to accept the bills, and then did some hard swearing in the preliminary proceedings to the effect that she had warned the good woman. The consequence was, she ran the double chance of being had up for perjury on her own account, or standing in the dock with her lord and master."

"Par nobile!" was Alec's comment.

"Well," continued Briggs, "the poor pedagogue was sold up, and he and his wife were turned adrift on the streets; while

Sam, who was made trustee to the estate, spent all the money in law expenses. The consequence was that the other creditors, who never got a sixpence, made common cause with the debtor, and prosecuted Sam for fraudulent trusteeship and conspiracy."

"Then it seems T. and P. must stand for Trusteeship and Perjury, not for Tea and Prayers any longer."

"Elsie Lund—her joke," said her husband.

"But the conclusion, my dear Briggs. Let us hear the end."

"The judge summed up dead against the prisoners, and——"

"What?"

"The jury not being able to agree on their verdict, were left consulting as the paper went to press."

"What a dreadful disappointment! We shall have to wait twenty-four hours before we hear the fate of our religious relatives."

"Pray, Elsie," said Alec, very seriously, "do not profane that beautiful word by applying it to those wretched people. We scarcely estimate the mischief we do by dignifying with the title of religion such a rhapsody of words as T. and P., just as we profane the word saint—one of the most expressive in our language—by making it a term of ridicule for Tartuffes and charlatans."

"The Reverend Alexander Lund," said Briggs, "evidently fancies he is back in Zoar, and orating at St. Simon Magus.' Do you know, between ourselves, I rather wish we were all of us back there."

"So do I."

"And I."

"And I."

"Let's go by the next train."

"Agreed."

"Let us take them by surprise," said Amy.

"Drop down suddenly and see whether Plantagenet is being properly taken care of," was Elsie's version of the same proposal.

" Bless that baby," said Briggs.

" Wait," ominously added Alec.

They took the train the very next morning, and considerably astonished everybody in Zoar by reappearing prematurely. They all went together to Topaz as a sort of head-quarters, and on bounding into Plantagenet's quarter Elsie found him being cared for far beyond her most sanguine expectations. Grouped around him were Mrs. Fane, Mrs. Wm. Llewellyn, and the nurse, while the infant himself was being dandled in the arms of none other than Mr. Moddle himself!

" Gracious goodness!" exclaimed Elsie, " what does this mean? Is the child ill?"

" Pardon the liberty, Mrs. Lund," said Mr. Moddle. " I've been all over the rest of the house, and when I came in here I could not resist the temptation of nursing your son and heir. I did the same with you once, you know."

" No apology is necessary. I'm glad to see you. Only you must really give me the baby for a little while. It seems ages since I saw him. You shall have him again in a minute or two."

When the nursery party broke up, and all reassembled in the drawing-room, Mr. Moddle explained that, lured by he knew not what attraction, he had felt an irresistible attraction to his old home in the Vicars' Close. He was getting an old man, and his wanderings had not thriven with him. Nature had evidently meant him for the scholar's life. So he had gathered around him the relics of his library, and invested what remained to him of his scanty resources in an annuity, which would supply his modest wants for the rest of his life.

" And have you quite abandoned all ideas of clerical work?" asked Alec—we must still call him by the old name; though here in the scene of his dignity it seems scarcely decorous to do so.

" On the contrary, clerical life seems to have abandoned me."

" Supposing Canon Wilcox saw the way to licensing the old Catholic Apostolic chapel as a mission room for relieving the congregation of St. Hilda's, do you think you could contemplate a sojourn in the tents of Anglicanism?"

" The thing of all others I should like," replied Moddle, quite catching at the notion.

" I really think it's a duty Mr. Moddle owes to himself, that he should accept such a position if offered," said Mrs. Fane.

" Why, dear madam?" Moddle always called Mrs. Fane " dear madam" now. It seemed to him a judicious fusion of affection and respect.

" Because then I should think you would have made the round of the sects," she answered.

" It's rather dangerous in this august assembly to speak of the Establishment as a sect, I should fancy," was the remark of Mr. Moddle.

" I shall suggest the scheme to Canon

Wilcox," Alec said; "and I think I can pretty well answer for the result."

"And I will go and secure the lease of my old house in the Vicars' Close. There are several to let there; but I should much prefer the one where I used to lodge, where for so many years I had the pleasure of teaching you, Mrs. Lund."

"Yes, that house must be very full of pleasant memories for you," replied Elsie, significantly.

"It is, indeed."

Then Mrs. Fane attracted the general attention by saying—

"Did I understand you that there were several houses to let in the Vicars' Close, Mr. Moddle?"

"Yes, dear madam."

"Why, mamma?" asked Amy.

"Because I should really like to settle in Zoar," answered Mrs. Fane. "There is nothing to attract me to town now Mr. Briggs has taken you from me, and one of the Vicars' Close houses would just suit me."

Briggs did not appear to hear Mrs. Fane's remark as to having filched away her daughter. He was at the pianoforte constructing an elaborate fugue out of an air which had just then begun to assume popularity. It's title was "Tommy, make room for your uncle."

"Briggs," shouted Alec, "don't you hear your mother-in-law's proposals ?"

But still that magic strain flowed on, "Tommy, make room for your uncle, there's a little dear !"

"No, I didn't hear anybody make proposals. Besides, it isn't Leap Year, my very dear madam—I mean mother."

"Be quiet."

"I can't—upon my life, I can't," he said, and retired to bury his mirth in the sofa-pillows.

Mr. Moddle opined that if his very dear madam really entertained ideas of a house in the Vicars' Close, the best thing she could do would be to honour him with her company so far, and then and there inspect one of those standing vacant. His very dear madam consented ; and off the two went to a fortissimo march by Briggs still on the same fruitful theme.

"Those two mean mischief, Amy," he said. "I think you had better go and act judicious bottleholder."

"Bless the old folks," was Amy's reply; "surely they can take care of themselves."

At this juncture William and Edward Llewellyn came in with the daily paper divided between them. As soon as they had passed the portal they each pulled a long face, but a face in which mirth was curiously blended with melancholy as they said—

"Poor Sam !"

"Poor Patty !"

"Is the case concluded ?"

"Look !"

The paper was handed round. It was a heavy sentence. The judge was determined to mark his sense of the enormity of their crime. He characterized it as slow murder, and felt that his duty would be to exile the male prisoner, at all events, for a period which would probably, at his age, be virtually banishment for life. Assuming that the female prisoner had acted under her husband's direction, he relegated her to a long period of imprisonment in her native land.

"It was a pity to separate them," said Alec, "but each will find a separate sphere for the really great abilities with which they are unquestionably endowed. Patty will start T. and P. among the female prisoners."

"More probably P. without the T.," suggested Elsie.

"Yes, possibly P. without the T.; and no doubt win the heart of the chaplain if only he happen to be evangelical; while Sam will, at the expiration of his sentence, instruct the aboriginal mind in the mysteries of sixty per cent., and the delights of mortgages and bills of sale. We all have our gifts."

When Mr. Moddle and Mrs. Fane returned, the announcement they had to make took nobody by surprise; it was a foregone conclusion. They discovered that two houses in the Vicars' Close were not necessary. By calling in the aid of Hymen one would amply suffice, and the joint incomes of Mr. Moddle and his now very dear madam indeed, would more than cover the modest rent and expenses of the joint messuage.

"But, mamma——" suggested Amy, at a subsequent discussion of the subject.

"But what, my dear? Now, please let me have no buts. You said very properly we were old enough to take care of ourselves. I guess what your but means."

"The religious difficulty. Is Mr. Moddle going to re-'vert to you, or are you going to re-'vert to him?"

"Neither one nor the other. We are going to illustrate the perfect possibility of two sensible people agreeing to differ on this subject. Canon Wilcox has made the offer at which Alec hinted; and Mr.

Moddle, with my full approval, has accepted it. We will be the Broadest Church people going here in Zoar. All the different forms of thought shall combine into one harmonious whole."

" All the two, as the French say."

" Are there only two ?"

" Look round, mother, you will perceive that you are the only dissentient."

" Then I will be the touchstone of your charity and toleration."

She was too. Very soon after the marriage the religious difficulty cropped up, and ever and anon—if we may look forward a little—it became a question whether the two houses in the Vicars' Close would not, after all, be required. By mutual concession, however, which often took a long time to bring about, and occasionally a brief retirement on the part of dear madam to the houses of her relatives and friends, the stormy married life of Mr. and Mrs. Moddle sped on towards the peaceful haven that lies out beyond for us all.

As for the rest of our little circle, it really seemed as if they had forestalled to some extent the peace of that future blissful condition. After all his weary wanderings, and fruitless beatings about in search of the truth, Alec Lund felt he had approached it as nearly as it might be possible amid the mists and darkness of this lower valley. He had realized at last the true ideal of life. He had congenial work and ample fortune, and by the time Plantagenet's little sister arrived to put her brother's nose out of joint, he felt as though he had been pastor of the poor East Zoar folks all his natural life.

Pastor Anglicanus, that was the title he kept before him as indicating the goal towards which his ambition tended—Pastor, not Presbyter, Anglicanus. The priestly element, if he grasped aright the genius and essence of the National Church, was in subordination to the pastoral. Gradually he put from him all other text-books of theology, and with his Bible in his hand he read, especially in the sayings of the Great Forty Days, the raison d'être, if so it might be termed, of National Churches.

But of the social rather than the theological aspect of what he did not in the least hesitate to call the Establishment he rather liked to speak. He had no objection to hear the Established Church spoken of as only one function out of many in a great moral police. This might not be its highest aspect, but it certainly was one ; and he was ready to strike hands with any, whether Romanists or Ranters, who would help him to keep his East Zoar people out of the public houses, their wives from the pawn-shops, their children from the gutter.

Canon Briggs and he actually inaugurated the preposterous notion that Church dignitaries might, could, and should work. Alec learned to sing a correct G and succeeded Briggs in the precentorship. As examining chaplain to the Bishop he had much to do with the training of the students at the Zoar theological college, and by drilling

them well in parochial work he not only
qualified them for their future positions, but
obviated the possibility of their loafing
about, as he remembered he and others had
done in their student days.

"If I had had parochial work to do I
should never have got into the mischief I
did, should I, Elsie?"

"You would certainly never have been
in your present influential position, you old
grumbler," replied his wife. "You would
have loafed to the end of the chapter."

"Beyond a doubt I should."

"And the Dean that was—the Bishop
that is—would never have taken you up if
it had not been for my Nicomachean Ethics
and Greek Tragedians."

"All of which you have shamefully neglected of late years."

"There is my moral philosophy," said the
proud young mother pointing to the cradle
where Elsie Secunda was sleeping.

"But there is your future Greek trage-
dian, my good wife," replied Alec, pointing

to Plantagenet. "He will very soon require his hic, hæc, hoc, and ὁ, ἡ, τὸ. I know I should pulverize him if I had to teach him."

"Poor Plantagenet!"

"Did you ever notice that the child does not look happy?"

"Often."

"A sort of morose look, utterly foreign to his nature, but there it is, is it not?"

"Yes."

"Do you trace a likeness?"

"Of course I do—poor Percy."

It is strange what freaks nature plays in this respect; how likenesses will leap over generations, or catch lineaments from far distant relatives.

"I have often wondered," Elsie continued, "whether we did our duty to Percy; whether, directly I found my heart wavering from him, I ought not to have told him, or told Uncle Edward."

"Of course I ought to have told your father. But we were young and thoughtless.

We see our duty now when it is too late."

"Poor Percy might have done better if we had acted more kindly by him."

Poor Percy! Surely if from beyond the dead man could have wafted a wish, it would have been thus he would like to be remembered. He had surmised in that last sad communication he had made to the living world that he should haunt Topaz as an unquiet shade. A very unquiet shade it was, as Plantagenet grew up daily more and more into the living likeness of his dead relative. A thing of joy and mirth, when by-and-by he flitted about the staircase, the fields, the gardens; and ever and again, when Elsie was initiating him in the mysteries of the alphabet, the strange, sombre look would steal across the child's face, and she would say, as she clasped him to her bosom—

"Poor Percy!"

The child was delicate, and often drooped. Whenever this was the case, Elsie made up her mind that he was going to die forthwith, and that his early fate was a punishment for her conduct to her cousin. Even Alec himself questioned, with his anxious heart, whether nature had not written the dead man's likeness on his ailing boy's face to chasten for the sins of his youth in the removal of him around whom the tendrils of his affection clung every day more closely.

"That child," he used to say, "first taught me to pray. I do not mean that I had not poured out petitions more or less formal to God before, but I never knew what wrestling in prayer meant until that dear child let me behind the veil. And that prayer prevailed. I care not what secondary causes you may allege. I give their due to careful physicians; I credit the fresh breezes of Topaz with all the efficacy I know them to possess, but that child is a Samuel—a child of prayer."

"I arn't Samuel, I'm Plantagenet," said the imp, indignantly.

He had quite repudiated the paternal

name which his sponsors had assigned to him in baptism, and assumed the lordly title which had been his own from birth.

"Suppose we call you neither Alec nor Plantagenet, but Percy," said his mamma.

"I don't mind Percy, but I won't be called Sam," answered the urchin.

"True," replied his father; "I had forgotten the inauspicious associations connected with Sam when I mentioned the scriptural name. Very well, my boy, you shan't be either Sam or Percy; you shall be Plantagenet, and nothing else."

There are some irreverent iconoclasts who denounce cathedrals as remnants of monasticism, and their dignitaries as drones. To such we would say,—Go to Zoar. There the cathedral seems to take its ancient position as the centre of good works, the veritable head-quarters of a mission always going on. From the Bishop down to the smallest chorister, there is a graduated scale of daily work usefully and cheerfully done.

His lordship had not learned to be

lethargic, even in the trying experiences of a decanal stall. He was a model working bishop, preaching all over his diocese the broadest of Broad Church doctrines, and startling the Lord Chancellor on his wool-sack by the advanced ideas he occasionally enunciated from his place in the House of Lords. His wife, who from the first asserted her independence by patronizing Miss Elsie Llewellyn in spite of the college antipathies to High Street, and notwith-standing Mrs. Grundy's assertion that she was a flirt, pursued the same line all along. The Episcopal Palace under her auspices became a regular Liberty Hall. She was of lofty birth herself, and therefore did not fear that dreaded thing called compromise so acutely as some bishops' ladies we have known, who, sprung from humble origin themselves, in days when their right reverend spouses were working curates, thought they must before all things be exclusive. Dean Wilcox and his wife were not quite of the same calibre; but good fellowship is contagious, and it is incredible what an effect it has upon the diocese in general and the cathedral town in particular when the Bishop and his lady can see their way to rising above the petty stiffness of episcopal starch.

The sight of sights to be seen in Zoar on a Sunday morning is the pair of Llewellyn brothers, Edward and William. They are brother churchwardens too of the parish of St. Simon Magus. The air with which they go arm in arm to church is edifying in itself; but when they are bolted in the capacious pew, lined with blue cloth and decorated with the insignia of their office, they form a magnificent embodiment of the command, " Let brotherly love continue." Who that saw them could guess through what exceedingly troubled waters *they* had arrived at this haven of rest and peace? Scarcely less instructive was the picture of their two wives. There was a time when Mary Ann thought Charlotte vulgar. The High Street element was even more distasteful to this genteel little woman than it was to the real big-wigs of the college and cathedral. Now they, too, started a quarter of an hour after their official lords and masters, and proceeded arm in arm to the same place of worship. Mary Ann had arrived at the dignity of a trumpet, and Charlotte had to talk a good deal louder than she liked—for she had never been demonstrative—in order to make her hear. Mary Ann made the wildest shots at her remarks, and, of course, answered ruinously wrong; but her companion bore it meekly, and said to herself, as she had said, if not in words in deeds, all her quiet life, along with Mr. Toots, that it " didn't matter."

At first Alec Lund was a little too learned for his simple flock at East Zoar; but gradually, as he used to say himself, he learnt by teaching.

"The pulpit," he would remark, "is a fine school for the preacher, even more than for the hearer. To see our words flying aimlessly over the heads of people who are so anxious to catch what is being said, forms the most appropriate punishment for us if we have the heart to appreciate it; if we have not that capacity we have no right in the pulpit at all. On the other hand, to see even the humblest listener following one's remarks and deriving comfort from what we announce is reward for the very loftiest."

"They don't seem to appreciate my sermons when I am in residence half as well as they do my inflected Litany or Tallis's Suffrages," said Briggs, who had never been great in the pulpit, and was inclined to dwarf even his own insignificant dimensions.

"And in that same Litany and those Suffrages I am, as you know, Briggs, always about a quarter of a tone flat. We all have our gifts. Let us say, 'For what we have received Providence make us thankful.'"

"What a fertile subject self is for parsonic conversation," said Mrs. Moddle, who happened to be present. "My dear Elsie, do you hear those exceedingly vain young dignitaries discussing their own merits——"

"And demerits," Elsie replied. "Let us be just."

"Their merits and demerits! What merits or demerits can they, as priests, have? The individuality of the priest with us is merged in the Church."

"Not at all a bad illustration of the difference in every respect between the Roman and the National Church, my very dear madam, as I know who used to call you," replied Alec Lund.

"Now we are in for an oration," said Mrs. Moddle, and arranged herself to listen resignedly.

"The three creeds may be very graphically described according to the prominence they give to the individual. In the bodies lying beyond the pale of the Establishment——"

"The Larger Church of England," suggested Elsie.

"The Larger Church of England, as those bodies are most appropriately termed—in these the individual is supreme. Mr.

Moddle, to wit, when angel of the Catholic Apostolic Church, or minister of the Baptist congregation, was the centre around which all the community gathered, and with the removal of which they vanished into thin air."

"A fortuitous concourse of atoms!"

"Hibernically speaking yes, my very dear madam."

"Don't, please."

"In the Established Church, while a good deal of this individual influence remains, it is no longer essential or supreme. The clergyman has a corporate as well as an individual existence. If I were to die to-morrow——"

"Alec!" said Elsie, deprecatingly.

"The next presentation would be sold to the highest bidder, and a weak-eyed curate put in to keep the place warm in the meantime," said Mrs. Moddle.

"In substance that is correct. The system does not break up with the man. Time was when I hated all systems and fretted at organizations——"

" Before you had a comfortable living?
That makes a vast difference."

" Possibly; though I am thankful to say
I am placed above the blandishments of
pecuniary piety. Now I think I see that
this system, this organization, is necessary
while religion is largely leavened with a
human element, and has to adapt itself to
the requirements of a highly material condition of civilization. I am still far from
thinking the parochial system the subject of
special inspiration, nor should I be at all
shocked if it were demonstrated to me to-
morrow that the Anglican succession was
hopelessly broken at the Reformation."

" Which, beyond doubt, it was," paren-
thetically observed Mrs. Moddle.

" I repeat, this would not affect me in
the least. The National Church as a whole
is exceedingly well typified by this cathedral
church of Zoar in particular. It is an
excellent system, and one which may be
developed into a thousand channels of use-
fulness, and against the use of which you

advance no argument by dwelling on its abuse. Cathedrals may and do develop lazy deans, carriage-lolling bishops, with no soul above nepotism, and canons who are very far from being big guns."

"Like our noble selves again!"

"But none of this can fairly be charged upon the system, no more than criminous clerks or tuft-hunters on the Establishment."

"But," once more urged Mrs. Moddle, "if you must have system, why not the perfection of system—Rome?"

"Because it is quite possible to have too much, even of a good thing. Because I submit to authority must I forfeit my individuality? To develop faith must I abjure reason? As soon would I confess that, to perfect the action of my leg I must cut off my arm, or to insure clear sight to my eye I must stop up my ears. No; the highest model——"

"Meaning me?"

“No; I did not intend a pun.—The loftiest ideal is one where all the faculties shall have free play, all work in perfect harmony.”

“Like my poor benighted husband’s eclectic Christianity!”

“There, the absence of all system, the undue prominence given to the personality of the minister, was the secret of collapse.”

“Ah, well,” summed up Mrs. Moddle, “you are a poor set. You do not exactly know where you are, I think. You have all changed about like a pack of weather-cocks. You and your mother Elsie are about the only ones in our immediate circle who haven’t ’verted. As for me, I say, ‘Write me down Catholic.’”

“So say I,” replied Mrs. Lund, “but it should be the largest catholicity of all, which stands embodied on Leigh Hunt’s tomb; ‘Write me as one that loved his fellow man!’”

“Write me,” concluded Alec, “when I pass

away from the scene of my labours, and you sit down with Plantagenet, Elsie, to pen an elegant Latin motto to follow my reverend name on the monumental brass in St. Simon Magus' church, write me down, ' Pastor Anglicanus !' "

THE END.